I0618882

CHIPLESS

THE CITY
BOOK 1

KFIR LUZZATTO

PINE 10

Pine Ten, LLC

205 N Michigan Avenue

Chicago, IL 60601

This is a work of fiction. Names, characters, places, and incidents are either the product of the author's imagination or are used fictitiously. Any resemblance to actual events, places, organizations, or persons, living or dead, is entirely coincidental.

First publication, May 2018

Copyright © 2018 by Kfir Luzzatto.

All rights reserved. No part of this book may be used or reproduced in any form without permission, except as provided by U.S. Copyright Law. For information, please address Pine Ten, LLC.

ISBN: 978-1-938212-71-0

CHAPTER 1

Kal gazed around him. He was nervous. Leaving the secured science complex to visit that uncivilized section of The City was adventurous and perhaps even reckless. He hoped to find a public H-cubicle nearby to connect his brain chip for a minute and calm himself. He already regretted having let Janec talk him into going outside.

Janec's Adam's apple, which always seemed disproportionate to Kal, now looked even bigger, and that irked him. Apparently, they didn't take that into account when matching Janec's parents. But then, even the Department of Guidance could make mistakes. Kal turned to his friend, who was waiting at the door for a couple ahead of them to get out of the way.

"I'm uncomfortable, Janec," he said. "Level Three technicians should not be in this part of The City."

"How many times do I have to tell you, Kal, that I have a permit?" said Janec, rolling his eyes. "Here, look," he added, pulling a little tablet from his breast pocket and waving it before Kal's eyes.

"Still, it doesn't feel right," Kal mumbled without looking at the permit. He swept his gaze around the room, avoiding eye contact with the customers. This place, which Janec had labeled "the best bar anywhere," was crowded with a colorful variety of low-level patrons. The room was large but so full that they were having a hard time pushing their way in. He was sure his Level 3 technician uniform made him conspicuous. It stood out in contrast to the rags that most people in the room were wearing. He hated being conspicuous.

Kal almost never left the safety of the science complex where he lived and worked. There was no reason for him to venture outside the well-guarded limits of the complex. He only passed through other sections of The City when he visited with his parents once a year. They lived in the best housing section, as befitting the parents of a gifted technician. But this was not a good neighborhood; it was Sector 5 of The City. Ordinary people lived in those streets. And the faces that he saw around the place were alien to him. They were unlike the quiet, serene people he met every day in the science complex. Here, everybody seemed to be uptight and even bad-tempered. How anyone could be like that when the chip did so much to keep everybody happy was more than he could understand.

"You need to unwind, Kal," said Janec, "after what you went through today...."

"Shhh!" Kal admonished him. "You can't talk about work here."

"All right, all right. Come on," Janec said, pulling him through a gap that had opened in the crowd. "I want you to meet someone."

"Meet? Who?"

"Come and see," Janec said. They had reached the end of the long room, and he started to climb a spiral staircase leading to the upper level. Kal noted with relief that the area upstairs was less noisy than downstairs. Subdued lights shone on chairs placed around small, round tables. Janec piloted them to a corner table on a balcony, from which they had a good view of the lower level.

"I'll be right back," he said, motioning Kal to sit down.

The upper level had its own counter loaded with bottles. Janec spoke to the girl behind the counter, a brunette dressed in tattered blue jeans and a flimsy shirt. Unconventional outfits seemed to be the convention in that bar. She walked Janec back to his table, carrying a bottle of yellow beverage and two glasses.

Kal jumped up to greet her, as his education required, and she gave him a smile mixed with a bit of laughter. She sat at the table and gave Janec an inquisitive look. She was slim but shapely, with a tomboyish haircut that seemed popular among the lower classes. Her green eyes, small nose, and full lips gave her a soft appearance.

"Kal, this is Amber," said Janec.

Kal sat down after a moment of embarrassed silence. "Nice to meet you, Amber," he said. "Do you work here?" he added, just for something to say.

"Sometimes," she said.

"Kal," said Janec, speaking in an undertone, "I was hoping that we could have an open conversation here. There are some things that I need to tell you—"

A noise from the lower level caught his attention, and he stopped. Five figures in white uniforms walked in, throwing the entrance door wide open and blocking the exit. Helmets with dark visors hid their faces.

"Immaculates!" Kal said with astonishment. "What can the High Professor's guard be doing here?"

Before anybody could comment, one of the uniformed men stepped forward and raised a hand. Everybody had stopped talking, and the room was in dead silence. The Immaculate pointed a large device he had taken from his belt at the head of a customer. A green light and a beep followed. The Immaculate moved the device from the first customer to the next with a sweeping motion. A red light blinked, followed by a blueish electric discharge that hit the man in the head. He fell to the ground, and an angry murmur rose from the people around them. The Immaculate addressed the crowd.

"Silence!" he ordered. "You have seen what happens to chipless criminals. If any other chipless individual is on the premises, he or she must step forward immediately. You know what happens to those who fail to comply," he concluded. He spoke with a flat, almost indifferent inflection. When nobody came forward, he went on talking. "We will now conduct a check of all those present. Stand still and wait for your turn."

"Amber..." said Janec.

"I'm out of here, don't worry," she said.

"I'll go down and show them the permit. That will slow them down. Besides, I don't want them to misinterpret our presence here when they see our Level Three uniforms. They may not know that Level Three technicians can visit this section of The City with a special permit," said Janec. "Wait here, Kal," he added, and he got up and sped down the spiral stairs.

"There is an emergency exit through that door," Amber whispered, speaking urgently. She had gotten up and was reclining on the table, out of sight from the lower level.

"No, thank you," said Kal. "It's all right. Janec is taking care of it."

"I wouldn't be so sure that it's all right if I were you. If you're smart, you'll leave immediately," she said. She threw worried glances over her shoulder to the floor below as she spoke.

"I'm fine. I'm a technician, and I'm here with a permit. Don't worry about me."

"Suit yourself," said Amber. She shook her head in resignation and left.

Kal watched as Janec approached the Immaculate, who seemed to be in charge. He spoke to him and showed him the permit. At that point, the discussion appeared to become heated. Kal couldn't hear what they were saying because of the distance and started to worry. Maybe Janec's permit wasn't valid after all. He watched as

Janec turned his head toward him and mouthed one clear word: "Run!" A second later, he fell to the ground, hit by a stun gun.

Kal stared in shock. He was at a loss to understand what was going on and why the Immaculates were treating his friend in that manner. However, one thing was clear to him: that girl, Amber, had been right. If they meant to treat him like they did Janec, he was in danger and had to flee. This wasn't the right time to clarify the misunderstanding. The Immaculates always followed instructions to a T, regardless of whether they were reasonable or not, and trying to reason with them was futile. He ran to the door through which Amber had disappeared, then down a flight of stairs and into the street.

The hot, stuffy air of the street hit him as he reached the pavement. He looked left and right. To the left, around the corner, was the bar entrance. Going that way meant running into the arms of the Immaculates, so he had to turn right into the darkness. He hoped to leave unnoticed and walk back to where they had left their vehicle. But the sound of boots behind him left no doubt that someone was chasing him. He ran as fast as he could into the small, dirty, dark alleys of that dangerous, lawless place. He didn't know where those streets were taking him. He also realized that he was lost and wouldn't know how to find his way back to the science complex once everything calmed down again.

CHAPTER 2

That day had begun like every other day in Kal's adult life. Getting up early, refreshed after a good night's sleep, he went into his apartment's H-cubicle to have his body parameters recorded. Checking the screen, he smiled, seeing that everything was green on the scale. In the old days, health control relied on sporadic, imprecise test methods that yielded unsatisfactory results. Modern medical technology, by contrast, allowed for continuous health control and management. It was a perfect fusion between the H-cubicle, which analyzed his health parameters every morning, and the chip in his brain. The chip controlled the impulses his brain sent throughout his whole body, according to the information it received from the H-cubicle. It was the chip that ordered the brain to make hormones and other chemicals needed for the body to function at its best. The H-cubicle checked the results of this work and provided feedback to the chip and to its owner. Kal always exercised and ate precisely according to the plan it displayed every morning.

He gazed out the window of his small but comfortable quarters, located in the technicians' area. Eating his breakfast while looking out at the green pastures beyond the science complex's walls was a wonderful, relaxing way to start the day. He particularly liked to watch the cows graze. It was a pity, he thought, that City residents had to stay within City limits, but he understood the wisdom of the law. It was important to avoid bringing dangerous pathogens into The City. He would have liked to see one of those animals close up, for once. Still, he was much luckier than the people who lived in Sector 5 of The City. Only a few lived close enough to the walls separating The City from the world outside to get a glimpse of that beautiful view. Most citizens only enjoyed a screened view of the rolling fields and of the animals outside. Since The Pulse, the biology of humans and animals had diverged so much that one could be dangerous to the other. The City had erected an invisible barrier to prevent birds and other flying creatures from coming into The City. It was also completely sealed by a physical barrier that kept animals out and humans inside. Still, it was some consolation that they could watch nature, even if only from afar.

Kal left for work, strolling along the path that went past the central square of the complex. At the square center, a statue of the High Professor watched with a benevolent smile over the buildings. Kal always liked to slow down and let the statue's gaze pass a sense of warmth onto him. *What a great motivation to start your work day*, he thought. All citizens owed their happiness to the High Professor. He was the genius who had perfected the chip implanted in every citizen on their first birthday. He had taken the initial prototype, developed by the first High Professor in the decades following The Pulse, and turned it into the technological marvel it was today. The original version of the chip had limited capabilities, but the High Professor had upgraded them. He had developed new chip software and methods for uploading it to the chips. Still, the latest chip types, like the one implanted in Kal's brain, were something else altogether. These new chips kept them healthy and improved their lives. Thanks to the chip, everything in The City ran smoothly and in an orderly fashion. Crime had disappeared, and nobody was helpless anymore. That, in reality, wasn't entirely true for Sectors 4 and 5, where some crime still existed, but that was an exception. If anything bad happened to you or your body, help was immediately available, right there in your head.

What's more, thanks to the chip, you always knew the right thing to do and the correct way to go. He smiled at the statue as if the High Professor could see him, and bowed slightly. The Professor deserved it.

A few paces after the statue, he met Aurora, who lived in a nearby building. She was a microbiologist, and Kal wondered if she would be his chosen mate. It was too soon to tell because the Department of Guidance, which dealt with mating matters, was always discreet. Still, some events hinted that she could be the one. For instance, their eating schedules were synchronized, so they met in the dining hall more often than not. Also, he had noticed that she was running into him more frequently. Her timid smile when their paths crossed seemed to speak volumes. But perhaps he was imagining things. He would have liked her to be the one, though. It was natural to start thinking about it at twenty-one, although he still had one year before the mating date.

Kal knew that he was handsome. Many in his generation were beautiful people as a result of the High Professor's outstanding mating policy. He was of medium height, slim but muscular, with blond hair, blue eyes, and a fair complexion. *A good fit for Aurora*, he thought.

He wondered how his parents would like her. He saw them only once a year, during the spring festival, and even then only for a day. That had been the rule since the beginning of his physics education when he was a bright student of fifteen. Sometimes he wondered if they would like to see him more often. But isolation from the family was a good thing—it allowed him to concentrate on his work without distraction.

During his last year of studies, he had come across an old

recorded lecture titled "Nociology: Negative Social Behavior." It described the weird, distorted social impulses people had before the invention of the chip. Many behaviors mentioned in that lecture were unthinkable by today's standards. For instance, people chose their mates at random, without any consideration of the result. They based their selection on a kind of physical attraction they called "love." That caused the decline of the race, with children of ill-fated matches growing up mentally diseased. Little wonder, then, that such a decaying society brought The Pulse upon them. And then, to compound the problem, they left procreation to the whim of the couples. It took place whenever a "desire" struck. That could happen at any time and for an unspecified number of times. Stupid. Today's matches, planned with scientific accuracy, avoided all that. And the procreation impulses, timed and delivered to the couple's chips by the Department of Wellness, ensured an optimal result.

At the physics building entrance, he gazed into the retinal scanner, and the door opened before him. It was a high-security building, complete with electronic eyes that followed him as he walked along the quiet corridors. He took the elevator to his office—a small cubicle with a computer terminal and a tiny desk. There, he picked up a tablet with the notes of yesterday's experiment and went on to his laboratory.

Kal loved his work. It made him feel that he belonged and was doing something worthy for his fellow citizens. He didn't mind that his research was limited in scope and that he didn't have the freedom to choose his own subject. He understood the importance of the topics assigned to him by the Department of Guidance. They contributed to the more extensive ABLOC research—the A Better Life for Our Citizens program—that ran under the supervision of the High Professor himself.

Kal had liked physics since he was a child. He had watched videos and programs that spoke about those topics. Therefore, the Department of Guidance's suggestion that he become a physicist had sounded just right to him. It was almost an inevitable career choice. Looking back, he couldn't recall having any doubts about the suggested assignment. His current project focused on improving a standard cardiovascular tester. That was one of the many subsystems embodied in the chip. It ran a microelectronic test on your cardiovascular system when you entered the H-cubicle.

While running some experiments the day before, Kal had come across unexpected readings and was eager to continue checking them. He so loved what he was doing that, left to himself, he would have remained at work even all night. That, unfortunately, was against the fifth rule of the Department of Wellness: "Workers shall not exceed five working hours during any working day." He always left his lab when the "Go home" message rang in his head. Now he was looking forward to continuing his experiment.

Kal's lab was on the fifth floor and had a nice window overlooking a rolling meadow. Multicolored flowers dotted the meadow year-round, and small birds fluttered overhead. His window opened only a little at the top. He liked to keep it open because of the spring scent of the meadow that reached his nostrils. He sat down to work, and time passed quickly as data accumulated on his tablet. He still had a few minutes left before leaving for the day, enough to check one more wavelength combination. This set was near the one that had given him abnormal readings the day before. He set the intensity of his wave generator to a low level and gazed at the results on his tablet. There were three wavelength ranges that he wanted to play with. He picked starting values for each, and then he turned the generator on. The simulator data remained normal, and he changed the wavelength of the intermediate signal.

Without warning, a blinding cascade of sparks appeared before his eyes, making him lose his balance. It lasted only for a second, but it made him dizzy and brought an acidic taste of nausea to his throat. His hand reached for the power button and turned off the generator. The dizziness subsided, and Kal, who had doubled up on the floor, was able to stand up. But he couldn't believe his eyes. What he saw through the window was incredible: the green meadow had disappeared, and instead he saw only brown-gray earth as far as his eyes could reach. Gone were the flowers and the birds, and instead of the sunny blue sky, he saw dark, menacing clouds. The air coming through the open slot in the window had an unpleasant, metallic smell.

Kal stood there, fighting nausea that still gripped him, gazing at the scene in disbelief, taking deep, slow breaths through his nose. In a few seconds, the scene changed again, bringing back the green, the flowers, and the birds that fluttered in the blue sky. The scent of the flowers reached his nostrils again, and he began to calm down. It took him only a minute to feel his old self again, although deep down, he was still shaken. It was time to leave, and for the first time since his graduation, Kal was happy to lock up his laboratory.

The science complex did not make it easy to meet other people. Also, the Level 3 rules did not allow socializing outside Level 3, so Kal didn't have many friends. Among them, Janec was the one he liked best because his field of research was close to Kal's, and he was easy to talk to. His office was in the same corridor as Kal's, so Kal stopped at Janec's door and knocked. When a "Come in" followed, he opened the door. His friend was at his desk, and without waiting for an invitation, Kal sat down in the only other chair.

"What's up?" Janec asked, lifting an inquisitive eyebrow. "You look troubled."

"I'm okay now, but I had this ... I don't know what to call it. For a moment, I felt that I was going mad. I'm afraid that something may be wrong with me. But it can't be. I've taken my weekly enhanced health test and scored very highly. I don't know what to think."

Kal went on to relate his experience to his friend, who listened in silence.

"Look, you may have overworked yourself," Janec said when Kal was finished. "You do that; I know it."

"I guess you're right. I've been working hard lately. I should slow down a bit."

"I'll tell you what you should do. Do you know what this is?" Janec asked, pulling a small tablet from his drawer.

"No. What?"

"This is my reward for being nice to that supervisor in Security. It's my permit to leave the perimeter of the research facilities by Gate Five, and you know what that means."

"What? You want to go downtown? To Sector Five? Why would you do that?"

"Because that's where the fun is. I've put the permit to good use several times, and I know that part of The City quite well. And the permit is for two, so I can take you with me. Go and log today's work, and we are good to go. I've already finished logging mine."

"Oh, I don't know. I've never been to that part of The City, and I don't feel comfortable going there. That's where the lower class is. It's not for us scientists to mix with them."

"Listen to me, Kal. You're a scientist, right? You can't make assumptions about something you've never tested for yourself. I am telling you that you are going to have the time of your life. It will take your mind off your bad experience. Don't make me beg. Go and get ready."

Kal hesitated. There was something in what his friend said. He needed a distraction. Besides, if he didn't like what he saw, he could always go back.

"All right, but on one condition: If I am uncomfortable, we come back immediately."

"Agreed," said Janec with a broad smile. "But you'll love it, I promise."

CHAPTER 3

Amber waited in the darkness of a narrow alley. A moment before ducking through the escape door, she had seen her friend Jamie run up the stairs. He knew which way to go in an emergency. He was sure to be coming along in a moment. Waiting was dangerous, but she couldn't leave Jamie behind. At last, she heard the sound of running feet. It had to be Jamie. The Immaculates never ran. It wasn't dignified. Instead, they used propulsion shoes to slide elegantly.

"Jamie," she cried, coming out from the shade. But it wasn't Jamie; it was Janec's friend, the dork who wouldn't run when she told him to. If he got that far and Jamie was not in sight, it meant that they had caught him, and he would not come. For a second, she considered backing away into the dark alley, but then, on an impulse, she went out into the open.

"This way," she cried, motioning to him to follow her.

This time, Kal didn't stop to think or argue and followed her into the alley. She ran so fast that he barely managed to keep up. Finally, she reached a door and threw it open.

"Inside!" she ordered, breathless. All that Kal could do was nod and follow her.

The door led to steep steps that took them underground to a passage lit by a subdued glow coming from the ceiling. They went up and down more steps and through more passages. They kept running until the last passage they reached led to a door. Going through it, they ended up in a small chamber poorly lit by a ceiling light. The chamber had a closed exit door. There, Amber stopped, leaning against the wall, panting. She closed the entrance door and turned a knob, locking it.

"We can stop here to catch our breath for a moment," she said.

"What—what happened?" Kal asked, still in shock.

The whole situation was overwhelming to him. He had followed her on the spur of the moment because he didn't know what else to do, but it was bewildering to him. For the first time, he got a close look at her—he couldn't help it in that small, crammed chamber. It made him uncomfortable. For one, her green eyes were too openly fixed on him, which, by The City's proper code of behavior, was a vulgar thing to do.

Furthermore, she had left the last button of her blouse unbuttoned. It was open at the top, showing some skin—something that women of his level would never do. The closeness imposed by the chamber's size was such that he felt her breath on his face. It was fresh and not at all unpleasant, but it was a constant reminder, breath after breath, of their improper physical proximity. Beads of perspiration ran down her neck, and Kal couldn't help smelling her body odor. Surprisingly, it wasn't unpleasant either.

"Did you see a boy in a blue shirt running up the stairs? Did you see what happened to him?" Amber asked, ignoring Kal's question.

"I think ... I think he may have fallen. I saw someone fall out of the corner of my eye, but I couldn't be sure. Who was he?"

"A friend," Amber answered after a brief hesitation. "A friend," she repeated.

"But ... what happened to Janec? You saw it. He had a permit for both of us. Why would they do something like that to him?"

"They must have found him out."

"What do you mean, 'found him out'?"

"Later. No time for that now."

Amber got up and opened the exit door that led from the chamber where they had stopped into what looked like a sewer.

"Wait a minute. Where are you going?"

"Listen," she said impatiently. "Stopping here for long is unsafe. I am moving on before those Immaculates find us. You can either go back to them or come with me. Whichever. Make up your mind," she added and started walking.

Kal hesitated for a moment. Everything was so foreign to his experience that he had no way to make an informed decision. But he understood that going back would be folly, at least until he found out what had sparked the Immaculates' unprovoked attack. He caught the door before it closed behind Amber and followed her.

"What are you doing?"

Kal had followed Amber in silence for half an hour, stepping where she stepped and doing what she did, but now her behavior no longer made sense to him. She was hitting a concrete wall with a stick, creating a rhythmic noise. Kal worried that she might be crazy.

"Shhh!" she said and continued to hit the wall.

A few seconds later, a section of the wall slid away, exposing a passage barely wide enough for a person to pass. Amber walked through it, and when Kal didn't follow, she turned to him.

"Get moving unless you want to remain outside!" she ordered. "The passage will close in a few seconds."

Shaken into action by Amber's call, Kal passed through the passage just before it closed. He found himself in a brightly lit corridor. Amber motioned him to follow her.

"Wait a minute," he said. "What is this place?"

"It's safety—or at least, as close to safety as we can get. I'll explain in a few minutes."

She turned away from him and started walking, and Kal followed her. As they reached the end of the corridor, a steel door opened, and a man appeared in the doorframe.

"Who's this? Where is Jamie?" he asked.

"The Immaculates got him. This is a friend of Janec's. He brought him to meet me, I don't know why, but before we could talk, the Immaculates arrived. Janec is down, and I don't know if Jamie is alive."

"Shit! What went wrong? Why would the Immaculates go there?"

"I don't know. Perhaps Kal can tell us. This is Kal," she said.

Kal gazed at them, completely bewildered. The man wore clothes more suited for a menial worker, but he spoke with authority. He was middle-aged, with graying hair that betrayed a slack adherence to health routines. A strange, antenna-like rod went from the back of his shirt to his head. It terminated in some kind of electrode that touched his skull. Kal had never seen anything like it.

The man seemed resigned upon hearing the news. He gazed at Kal for a second and then said, "Come inside," and moved aside. "Inside" was a large room with three other men busy with some electronic equipment. They also wore the strange antennae. Two giant screens were dark, and the place had no windows. The maze of corridors they had followed had many stairs going down, which meant they had to be deep underground. Now that he had time to observe, Kal felt claustrophobic.

The stranger walked to a corner and motioned for them to sit on a bench. He dragged a chair from another corner and sat before them.

"I'm Seth," he said, extending a hand for Kal to shake. Kal took it and shook it in silence, waiting for Seth to continue.

"So, you got yourself in trouble," he said at last.

"I don't know how. I didn't do anything wrong. I have no idea why the Immaculates acted as they did and why they chased me. I don't know what to do next, either," he added in despair. "Anyway, what is this place? What are you doing here?"

"That's a lot of questions, isn't it?" said Seth, smiling for the first time. "Let me try to answer them. First of all, you should know that your name is not new to us."

"It isn't? Who's 'us'?"

"Slowly, boy." Seth turned his attention to Amber. "Did you tell him anything about this place?" he asked.

"Nothing. We were too busy running. No time or breath to speak."

"Good. I'll start from the beginning, then. There is a term that you haven't heard before because the High Professor banned it many years before you were born. The term is 'augmented reality.' Do you know what it means?"

"I never heard it, and I don't understand its meaning. Reality is reality, and you can't add to it," said Kal.

"Oh, yes, you can. We'll come to that in a minute. Like most people and me, they implanted you with a chip on your first birthday. Those who, for any reason, don't have the chip are outlaws and are either imprisoned or killed on sight."

"Yes, I know, and I saw it happen today. But what kind of barbaric individual would give up the privilege of a chip? It doesn't make sense to me."

Amber, who was sitting on the bench next to Kal, touched his arm. "I don't have a chip," she said, sounding teasing. "Do you think I'm a barbarian?"

"Uh, no! I mean ... why don't you? Oh, I don't understand ... I'm sorry," said Kal, obviously embarrassed.

"Let's take this one step at a time, Amber. Don't go confusing him," Seth rebuked her.

"All right. Sorry," she said, but she didn't look genuinely sorry.

"The best way to explain this is to show you. Come with me," he said, getting up. "You too, Amber."

A short walk to another door in the room led to a corridor that ended at an elevator shaft. The three of them mounted the elevator platform at the bottom of the shaft. Seth pushed a button, and the elevator took them up to a point where a steel lid blocked the passage. Pressing another button opened the lid, and the elevator continued to climb.

"Do you know what year this is, Kal?" Seth asked.

"Of course; it's the seventy-fifth year of the chip revolution."

"But the world didn't begin with the chip, right? There was life before then."

"But that was before The Pulse," Kal pointed out.

"Yes. Our civilization is an ancient one. If we hadn't stopped counting with The Pulse, the year now would be 2127. Can you imagine what such a civilization produced in so many years? These structures date to before The Pulse—I don't know how long before it. That's how advanced our ancestors were at the time. We started fifteen floors underground, and I'm taking us to the surface," Seth said.

The elevator stopped at the top of the shaft, and Seth keyed in another combination on its keyboard. A section of the shaft moved, revealing a beautiful view. A rolling pasture was dotted with sheep, flowers, and trees. Birds chirped all around the shaft, and the sun shone high in a cloudless sky.

"Isn't this a perfect pastoral view?" Seth asked.

"It is, indeed," Kal agreed. The mere sight of the beautiful scene infused him with a kind of peace and serenity.

"Have you ever wondered why The City has walls through which we cannot pass? Or how it is that you can see the outer world from afar, but you cannot go there?"

"Nothing to wonder about. I know the answer. As a result of The Pulse, our ecosystem has diverged from that of other crea-

tures, and contact between man and animals has become dangerous. That's why we don't mix."

Seth shook his head without commenting on Kal's answer. He
unbuttoned his shirt and removed the backpack it covered,
together with the antenna-like device.

"Here, put this on," he ordered.

"What is this for?"

"You'll see in a minute," said Seth. "It's off now, but let me
explain before I turn it on."

He helped Kal tighten the backpack's straps and then short-
ened the telescopic antenna until the electrode touched Kal's head.

"So here is the thing," said Seth. "You see all the green grass,
the sheep, birds, and all that, right?"

"Of course; why shouldn't I?"

"Because they don't exist. What you see is augmented reality.
You see what the High Professor wants you to see, not what is out
there."

"That's nonsense. Of course it's all real!"

With a sad smile, Seth touched the backpack and switched
it on.

CHAPTER 4

Kal pushed himself up from the floor. He was still on all fours where he had dropped, too dizzy to stand. He felt nauseous, but he had to look again. Slowly, his gaze followed Amber's and Seth's legs until it reached the height where the transparent section began. Seth's hand grabbed his and helped him to his feet. He looked out again. The green grass was gone. There were no sheep, no birds, or trees. Thick, dark gray clouds hid the sun. Nausea grew in Kal's throat again, and he had to slide down and sit on the floor.

"What ... what happened?"

Seth touched the backpack and switched it off.

"Now you can look again," he said.

Kal gazed out, relieved to see the grass and the sheep back again.

"I don't understand," he said.

"You will, but let's go back inside first. Staying out here may be dangerous."

Inside, Seth took the backpack away from Kal. They sat again, and Amber offered him a carafe with a cold liquid, and he drank avidly. It was freshening and a bit alcoholic. Kal didn't like alcohol much as a rule, but this time he appreciated the boost it gave him.

"That was ... uncanny. It was like what happened to me at work this morning. I can't figure out how it happened. When everything disappeared, and all I saw was desolation ... are you saying that's what they call 'augmented reality'?"

"Quite the contrary. What you saw was real. The rest—the sheep, the grass, the birds—that's all imagination. That's augmented reality."

"But ... but I don't understand. Can you explain it to me?"

"The City is dying, Kal. That's what is happening. Before The Pulse, more than nineteen million people lived here. Now it's less than three million. The tyrants who govern us—the so-called High Professor and his gang—are recycling the dwindling resources of The City. They keep The City going this way, with help from goods they get from outside. They keep all contacts with the outside world secret. The Immaculates supervise all commercial transactions, and nobody else knows about them. Even they cannot speak with people from the outside. The exchange of goods takes place through automatically sealed compartments. The Immaculates and the sellers from outside never meet in person. 'For protection against diseases' is the excuse that the government gives for it. The reality is that the flow of information is what they fear.

"But all that can only support an increasingly smaller number of people. That's why they must control the birthrate. Their criterion is one: every newborn has to be manageable via the chip. They turn everybody into unwitting slaves, and they keep us from knowing the truth. There is a whole world out there, one you don't know about. You think that it is poisonous to the extent that going there would kill you, but that's a lie. Letting us know the truth would mean losing control over us and would be the end of the High Professor's rule."

"I ... this is incredible. It goes against everything I know. I will need more information before I can accept what you are saying."

"I'll tell you all I know. But first, you were saying you experienced reality at work this morning. Tell us about it."

Kal related his experience with the combination of wavelengths. As soon as he finished his story, Seth got up and started pacing the room, excited.

"This is great! It is huge! You don't understand how important it is—and you are."

"No, you're right. I don't."

"Look, the High Professor rules us. He rules us by controlling our chips. He can broadcast anything he wants to us, and that's what we will see, feel, and think. Each one of us. He also rules us via the H-cubicle, the health cabinet that he so 'generously' gives every citizen. He decides who learns what, who marries whom, and what you will like to eat, watch, or do. To keep us happy, he broadcasts images of a perfect world, so we don't realize that we live in a cage—a huge, decaying cage. He lets us think that we are living a wonderful life."

"But that's horrible! So why don't you remove the chip if it's so bad?"

"You have seen with your own eyes why. If you are chipless, you're as good as dead. Have you ever heard of TCE? No? It's our name. It stands for 'The Chip Enemies.' We are a small group of scientists who have decided to rebel against the tyranny of the High Professor. I am a chip engineer by training. I have developed the neutralizer that we all have on us, which you have seen in action. We need it so we can see reality for what it is."

"But why keep it on at all times?"

"I'll explain. How well do you know the topography of The City?"

"I know about the five sectors, in general, but the only part I know well is the science complex where I live ... lived."

"The five sectors are the populated areas. That's a tiny part of the original city. The epicenter of The Pulse was far away from here, but the electromagnetic storm it generated reached this place. That wreaked havoc on the original city's infrastructure. It caused fires, explosions, and extensive destruction. The uninhabited part of The City is ten times the combined area of the five sectors. Its borders are close to Sector Five. That's where we are now, at the edge of the wreckage and just outside Sector Five. I've never been farther inside the ruined part of The City, but those who went there tell me that it is immense."

"But what about the neutralizer?"

"The Immaculates don't know exactly where we are, but they have a pretty good idea of the area where we hide. They don't come close because this is an ancient atomic energy facility, and they fear the danger of radiation. We have dropped a small amount of radioactive material outside to keep them away. The radiation isn't strong enough to reach underground, so there is no danger to us. Still, it is detectable outside, so the Immaculates don't come too close. But they have tried to get to us by broadcasting high-intensity augmented-reality signals that should scare us off. Last time, it was an invasion of rats that would eat us alive. They even added the illusion that one of us was being eaten. Very scary. But when we fear something like that, all we have to do is turn on the neutralizer. It's uncomfortable to keep it on us at all times, but there is no other way. Until now, at least."

"Why? What happens now?"

"Now you may have the answer. Our neutralizer only works if the antenna is in contact with the skull. It has to be near the chip's location, so we need to have one for each person. There is no way that we can manufacture millions of neutralizers and teach everybody how to use them. You've seen how hard it was for you to come to terms with reality. But if you can broadcast a neutralizing composite wave, that's the answer. Then we could show the reality to the entire population and end the High Professor's rule. That's our dream. Can you teach us how to do it?"

Kal shook his head in sorrow.

"In time, I might. But I would need to do much more research. All I've accomplished by accident was an effect that worked at close range. To do a wide-area broadcast, I would need much more than that. What I know is a start, but no more than that."

Seth nodded.

"I see. Yes, that's logical. We'll need to give you the equipment and the time if you are with us. Are you?"

Kal turned pensive. The last hour had been enough to revolutionize the way he saw his world. It had turned it upside down, from a serene, well-organized, and secure life into one that had no sure tomorrow. And now they were asking him to become a revolutionary.

"I ... I need a moment to think about all this," he said.

"Of course. This must have been a shock to you. I remember how dumbfounded I was when I discovered that I had been living a lie," said Seth.

"Thank you," Kal murmured.

He got up and walked to the far end of the room. There, the lighting was more subdued, and he felt far enough from the others and the pressure their explanations were putting on him. He needed some solitude to think coherently. Even assuming everything they said was true, he wished he had never learned it. He liked his quiet, uneventful life and his work. Now all that had been taken away from him, probably forever. There had to be a way out, he said to himself. But going back to his former life as if nothing had happened wasn't a real possibility. There was no escaping from that conclusion. Resigned, he turned around and faced Seth again.

"I'd like to help," he said, "but the Immaculates are looking for me, and I don't know what will happen if they catch me. I couldn't hide here because I can't do this kind of research underground. Anyway, I would need a sophisticated laboratory, equipment, and a large testing area, which I assume are not available here. It doesn't look doable to me. I'm sorry."

"There is a place where you could do it. We have support from the outside world; otherwise, we would not survive. We have relations with a faraway place where you could do it, but of course, you need to get there first. Amber?" said Seth.

"What?"

"Would you take him?"

"What, now? You know what I'm here for."

"I know, and I understand how important it is to you. But this ... this may change our world. It may be our dream come true, and there is nobody better positioned than you to do this—you know that."

"So, you want me to go back and forget what I have come for? Are you really asking me to do that?"

"This is bigger than you and me, Amber. Besides, our days here are numbered. They have Janec and Jamie, and they know where we are."

"But didn't you cancel that data from their chips?"

"I did," said Seth, "but there are other ways to get at it."

"So we go away. We move to another location," Amber argued.

"There is no other safe location for us, Amber," said Seth. "We would need to go outside, explore, and find another place. The moment we go aboveground, our chips can be located, exposing us, and they'll get to us in no time. No, we must stay here and hope that they won't find us. But you—you have a place to go. And a mission that may be the most important ever. And if you succeed, you will also get what you came here for. You understand that, right?"

"All right. I'll take him. I'm not happy about it, but I'll take him." Turning to Kal, she added in a low voice, "Go get some sleep. We'll have to get going soon, and Seth and I need to plan."

"Amber is right, Kal. You need to rest. You had a hard day. Take one of the empty cots—anyone you like. You have a long walk before you."

Seth's hand shook Kal awake. He had had trouble falling asleep at first, but then fatigue had overcome him. He didn't know how long he had slept and had no means to tell in that place, but he felt rested.

"Good morning," said Seth. "Let's go and sit at the table over there. We'll have some breakfast, and then we need to bring you up to speed on what Amber and I have planned."

Kal sat up on the bed and looked around him.

"If you're looking for an H-cubicle, we don't have one here," said Seth with a smile.

"Oh, no. I was only trying to orient myself. All this is so strange—"

"I understand. We have a washing cubicle over there where you can freshen up—no electronics there, though."

Kal used the washing cubicle, after which, feeling more awake, he joined Seth and Amber at the table. It was a coarse wooden table such as he had never seen before, and he ran his fingers over the surface, feeling its texture.

"Are you with us, Kal?" Amber asked, seeing that he was furrowing his brow and concentrating on the tabletop.

"Yes, sorry. What do you want me to do?"

"Eat," said Seth.

They ate in silence, standard fare not unlike Kal's daily rations, except for the bread and cheese, which looked too alien to him to try. After a while, Seth pushed his plate away and spread a plastic map over the table.

"Look at this, Kal. We are here," he said, pointing with his finger. "You need to get there," he added, pointing again. "This place is Freeland. Amber will explain more about it later. Between here and there, you first have the Surroundings. That's a narrow strip of land that is quite populated. It maintains a commercial relationship with The City. Beyond the Surroundings lies a huge, dangerous, scarcely populated territory. But you don't need to worry about that, because the plan is not to cross it on foot. Airlifting will be arranged. Amber will tell you all about it. I don't want to waste time now going into too many details. Every hour that passes makes it more dangerous. If the Immaculates are set on catching you, the sooner you're out of here, the better. Questions?"

"I have so many that I don't know where to start. To begin with, how do we get out of The City without being caught?"

"One of the reasons that we have turned this place into our headquarters is its location. The corridor through which you came is part of a network of tunnels that extends beyond the city's walls. That's how you'll leave."

"I see. How long will it take us to get out of The City limits?"

"It depends on how fast you walk, but you should get out in less than twelve hours. We have prepared some supplies for your trip. It's all in the rucksack, and I'll add the map in case you need it later. We have kept it as light as possible because you'll have to carry it for quite a distance."

"All right, then; I don't have any more questions right now."

"I have a question," said Amber. "What kind of name is 'Kal'?"

"It's short for Kallias," said Kal, blushing. "It's the name of an ancient hero, or so my mother told me."

"A hero, good," said Amber, sneering. "That's exactly what I need for this trip."

CHAPTER 5

Kal took a break to wipe sweat from his brow and to drink a little water. They had walked in what looked like an endless tunnel for close to five hours, and he was starting to feel tired. Amber, in contrast, was pushing forward at a steady pace despite the heavy rucksack that she was carrying. True, Kal's was heavier, but she was smaller.

"Why are you stopping?" she asked without looking at him.

"We need to rest a little and to eat something. How much farther do we have to go?"

"We're almost halfway, I think. Yes, let's sit down and eat," she agreed. "This part of the tunnel is really hot," she said, and she took off her blouse, under which she wore a flimsy tank top. "Later it will get cold as we go deeper into the ground, but right now, I'm sweaty."

She sat next to him, opened her rucksack, and searched through it by the weak light of her flashlight. They had set it to a low level to save energy. "If we run out of light in that tunnel," she had explained, "we'll get lost."

"What is this place?" Kal asked.

"It's actually a maze of underground passages. Nobody knows their origin. I heard that they are part of an underground military installation built centuries ago. In any case, the one tunnel that I know well will take us outside the borders of The City."

"How can you be sure that we are heading in the right direction? If there is more than one tunnel, we could be walking in the wrong one."

"Did you see the symbol on the wall, the one with the eagle head? It is printed at every turn. Other tunnels have different symbols. That's how I know."

Kal gazed at her for a moment and then looked away. He was having a hard time understanding the ease with which she exposed parts of her body. In The City, the most he had seen of a woman was her neck, and even then, he had properly refrained from staring at it.

"What?" she asked.

"Nothing."

"Nothing? You look like you've seen a monster."

"No, really. It's just ... that thing on your shoulder. It's a tattoo, right?"

"Yes, why?"

"It's unhealthy. City people don't get tattoos. They're illegal."

"Screw city people, then. I like mine."

Kal remained silent for a minute, looking at the tattoo with fascination.

"That's a sun in a circle, right? What does it mean?"

"Nothing."

"Nothing? That doesn't make sense. You don't blemish your body with something that means nothing."

"Nothing, I said." She said it in a way that did not invite more questions.

Amber took a loaf of bread from her rucksack and broke it in half. She gave one-half to Kal and then did the same with a piece of cheese. Kal took the food and examined it at length. He had never eaten anything that didn't come from a sanitized food repository. He couldn't help wondering what eating under such unhealthy conditions might do to his body. The thought didn't leave his mind as he watched Amber eat with gusto. But then, he reminded himself, she was chipless, almost a barbarian.

"Are you planning to eat it or to get nutrition by gazing at it?" Amber asked with a mocking smile.

Kal blushed, pecked at the cheese, then at the bread. They both tasted great, and he took a real bite.

"It's good," he said with a full mouth.

Amber gave him a side glance and said nothing. Kal chewed on his food and began to grow annoyed by her apparent disdain. He felt as though she was disgusted by everything he said. As he continued eating, his irritation grew. He had to say something. After all, they were partners on a dangerous trip. He finished his food in silence and drank avidly from his canteen.

"What do you have against me?" he asked at last, without looking at her.

"Why, nothing," she said, speaking casually.

"Not true. You've been treating me as if I have done something wrong. I can sense your hostility."

"It's not that. It's complicated," she said.

"Then explain it to me."

Amber remained silent for a minute, and then she turned toward him and looked him straight in the face.

"All right. I'll tell you. Your discovery—if that's what it is, which I don't know for sure yet—has ruined my plan. Everything I've been working for in the last six months."

"Why? How could I?"

"As Seth told you, I come from far away, from Freeland. That's where we are going. Getting here wasn't easy, but I was determined to do what I came for. But to succeed, I had to stay in The City, and now I can't because I need to take you to where you can do your experiments."

"But why you, then? Why can't somebody else take me if it's so important for you to stay in The City?"

"I'll tell you some other time," said Amber, getting up. "Now it's time for us to get going, or we'll never see the end of this tunnel."

Kal got up and followed her in silence.

———————

"Is there a problem?"

Kal had stopped and was leaning heavily against the wall.

"I think ... I have lost the base signal. My chip isn't receiving any more. I felt it happening for a while now, and it's weird."

"But that's a good thing, right? You're no longer under the influence of the High Professor. We have walked far enough that they can't control you. You are a free person for the first time in your life."

"Yes, but you don't understand. The base signal is that which gives us the feeling of well-being."

"A fake well-being," Amber retorted.

"There is no fake or non-fake feeling of well-being. Once you feel well, that's all there is to it. Now that the baseline is gone, I am confused. It feels different, strange. I need to rest for a while."

"All right. Sit here, and I'll go a little farther to see if I can find a shortcut. My map says that there should be one nearby. Meanwhile, use the time to rest."

———————

Left alone in the semi-darkness, Kal dropped his rucksack and sat beside it. He felt empty and lost, as if a part of himself had been cut away. He sat there, eyes closed, but a voice made him sit up.

"Amber?" he called, but the tunnel was silent, and she wasn't anywhere in sight. Still, he was sure that he had heard her voice.

Was the solitude getting to him, making him hear things? *Where is that stupid shortcut?* a voice said in his head. *Oh, well, it's probably not as close as I thought; I'll go back*, it continued. Kal started to panic. This was terrifying. It had to stop. A mental picture of Amber's voice formed in his mind. It had an elusive shape, full of dancing colors and waves, but it became something tangible in his mind. He knew that he could touch it and change its shape. He concentrated on the mental image of Amber's voice. He imagined it shrinking until it fell silent, and he realized he had blocked it out. The wavy, colorful image was still there, dancing in his head, but he knew how to control it. He allowed it to grow a little, and Amber's voice came back for a moment before he shut it out again. Now all he heard was the silence of the tunnel. But he had heard it. And it was Amber's voice; that much was clear. What was happening to him? Was it the loss of the signal that was driving him mad?

Kal stood there with a furrowed brow, trying to make sense of what he had experienced. Slowly, an explanation presented itself, one that was incredible but possible. Telepathy! He was actually hearing Amber's thoughts—either that, or he had gone crazy. Transmission of electromagnetic waves was his field of work, and he understood waves. That was what the High Professor's transmitter did for everybody in The City. The chip received even very weak signals, but only those meant for it. The chip's receiver filtered out any other electromagnetic signal. It had to be that way; otherwise, the chip would be flooded with irrelevant signals and would not function properly. Kal understood the underlying science well. But now, it seemed that his chip had lost specificity. It was receiving electromagnetic waves originating from Amber's brain. *How is that possible?* he wondered.

He started to pace up and down the tunnel, thinking hard about his experience, and that's how Amber found him. He was so deep in thought that he almost rammed into her and only noticed her at the last moment.

"Is this your way of resting?" she asked.

"Listen. I need to know if I'm going mad. Listen to me, okay?"

"What's the problem?"

"I heard voices in my head. Only for a moment after you left, I heard someone saying, 'I hope he's not going to crack,' and then silence. Did you say that? Did I hear you say it?"

"No, I didn't say it—"

"So that's it. I'm going mad! It must be the chip doing that to me because I've gone out of range." Kal started to tremble at the thought of the consequences.

Amber placed a hand on his arm to stop him from shaking. "I didn't say it, but I thought it. How could you know what I was thinking?"

Kal stood there with a furrowed brow, looking for a simple way to explain it to her, but more importantly, to himself.

"When I had that event, back at the lab, I saw the reality for the first time. The electromagnetic waves I generated must have altered the inner structure of my chip. Apparently, I have ruined its filter, so now it receives signals at a different wavelength. Human brains broadcast electromagnetic signals all the time, but they are weak. So far, nobody has developed a receiver capable of decoding those signals. Some people's brains have an extremely rare innate ability for natural telepathy. But the power of the chip is far greater than that of the human mind. That must be it!"

Kal's voice reflected the excitement he felt as a scientist.

"Do you mean to say that you can hear everything that goes on in my head? But that's awful!" exclaimed Amber.

"No, don't worry. I can turn it off. In fact, I must turn it off because otherwise, I'd go crazy hearing other people's thoughts all the time. Now it's only you and me, but I don't know what will happen when I'm in a crowd. Anyway, I'm not hearing anything right now, but let me try to see how well I can control it. Wait a second! Yes, now I can hear you. You thought that you felt exposed, right?"

"What do you want me to do now? Stop thinking?" she blurted in anger.

"No, I'll switch it off. I feel uncomfortable when it's switched on, and I can't keep it going for long. And then we need to be close enough for me to receive. When you walked away, it stopped. Don't worry, I won't eavesdrop on you."

"Uhmm, I'm uncomfortable all the same. You're a freak."

"I'm sorry."

"So am I ... that I'm stuck with a mind reader," Amber concluded. She remained silent for a few moments, and then, as was her nature, she became practical. "Tell me, can you also project your thoughts to somebody else? Because if you can, that would be useful. We could speak in that way when other people are around."

"I don't know. This never happened to me before. I have no experience."

"Then try it," she said, now sounding excited that her idea might work.

"How?"

"How would I know? Think of something simple, something that I can be sure is your thought, and try to get it to me. I'll tell you when I get it."

"Okay, I'll try," said Kal.

Amber closed her eyes to concentrate and listen.

"I heard nothing," she said, opening her eyes after a full minute passed in silence, "and ... Eek!"

"What happened?" Kal asked, alarmed.

"There!" Amber said, pointing farther down the tunnel.

"What? There's nothing there."

"What, can't you see it?"

"See what?" he asked.

"A dog. Wait a minute—were you thinking of a dog?"

"Yes, yes! A big, brown dog." Kal was excited.

The dog disappeared.

"Now I get it," said Amber. "Unbelievable! You didn't send the words 'big brown dog' to me, but instead, you made me see the image that you had in your head."

"It's augmented reality in reverse! That's what I would see if The City transmitted the image of a dog to my chip. Instead, I must have ruined the circuits of my own chip so badly that it generates augmented reality and projects it to chipless people. That's amazing!"

"I've said it, and I'll repeat it—you're a freak."

"I surely turned into one. I don't know what I would give to get to that Freeland of yours, have the chip removed, and get a chance to study it. What I can learn from it is precious."

"I, for one, will be happy when they get that thing out of your head," declared Amber. "One can't feel comfortable around you as long as it's in there."

"I'm sorry. Making people uncomfortable is against my upbringing. I would like you to feel comfortable in my company."

"Well, we don't always get what we want," said Amber, arranging the straps of her rucksack. "I want to forget this thing for now. It's time for us to get going. But if you eavesdrop on me, I'll know it. I won't envy you if you do."

Kal nodded and followed her in silence. There was nothing more he could say.

———— · —— · ————

The following five hours passed slowly, with Amber and Kal walking in silence. The temperature of the tunnel dropped as they advanced. They walked for two hours without saying a word. Kal was worried by Amber's silence and whether it meant a deterioration in their already rocky relationship. He had had to fight the temptation to open his mind to her thoughts. They had reached a segment of the tunnel where the temperature had risen again. The exit had to be near, but after a while, Amber stopped abruptly.

"Oh, no!" she said in dismay.

"What's the matter?"

It was the first time that Kal had heard her sound concerned. They had reached what looked like the end of the tunnel. Huge steel doors blocked their path.

"They sealed the exit. I can't believe it!" she said, shaking her head.

"What do you mean, 'sealed'?"

"The Immaculates always search for underground entrances to The City. When they find one, they seal it to avoid uncontrolled access. This is the one I used coming in, and it was well concealed. I didn't dream that I wouldn't be able to use it to get out. Now we're in trouble."

"But perhaps we can open these doors," Kal objected.

"Look at them. They are welded together. To open them, we would need heavy equipment that we don't have."

Kal inspected the doors more closely and saw that she was right. The metal had been recently melted.

"We have to go back, then," he said.

"No. let me think," she said.

Amber sat on the floor and rummaged through her rucksack. After a minute, she pulled out a piece of paper and held it high in her hand.

"I knew I had it!" she said with evident satisfaction.

"What is that?"

"Look here," she said, unfolding the paper on her lap. "This is a map of the tunnels that Afex gave me before I left for The City— Afex is the one we are going to see. I'll tell you about him later. It shows alternate routes into the maze that I would have used to get in if this one were closed. This is the best, but there are others. See this one here? It goes down a few levels and then comes up near the exit, so it's more walking for us, but if it's open, we can get out."

"*If* it's open," Kal commented. "And what is this blue line between this tunnel and the other one?"

"It's an underground river. We'll have to cross it to get to the other tunnel."

"We are not equipped for water crossing," Kal objected. "We may be stuck there."

"We'll find out when we get there. Do you have a better idea?"

Kal shook his head. Amber got up. "Let's go, then," she said.

CHAPTER 6

Professor Larkin was the powerful head of the Immaculates. He wasn't a professor of anything; that was only a title given him to keep him in character with the ruling caste, headed by the High Professor. He owned the Immaculates in every sense. Every year, Larkin personally picked 100 five-year-old boys to join the Immaculates' academy. He selected them based on a detailed character analysis done through their chips. Being selected meant severing ties with their families. From that moment, Larkin functioned as their father, mother, and personal God. The boys were groomed and trained to be totally unshakeably loyal to Larkin. The system monitored every second of their lives and decided who would become officers among the best cadets.

Fewer than 300 officers were instructed in the secrets of The City's management, including the power of augmented reality. They were the only ones allowed to go outside The City limits, and even they could only go on special missions. They would die for Larkin or the High Professor without hesitation. They manned a fleet of two hundred flying platforms equipped with heavy weapons. So far, there had never been a need to use it, but it was ready to protect The City against any possible external menace.

In the hours following the incident at the bar, Larkin had remained at headquarters. He paced his office nervously, waiting for news. Since his control system had flagged the report that young physicist Kal had logged, he had been on edge. The tentacular computer system that ran The City's information infrastructure was quite sophisticated. It analyzed all the information collected into the central memory and generated a map of individuals who exhibited deviant behavior. It analyzed every sentence with powerful natural language software to flag potential anomalies. The Immaculates checked every alert meticulously. They usually turned out to be false alarms, and this was the first troubling case in more than a year.

At first, it looked like a harmless report, something that would not deserve more than a routine check. After all, the technician had filed a report to the system. It detailed some strange effects that an electromagnetic discharge had on him. He attributed it to a momentary ailment that affected his vision and indicated that the man was not ill-intentioned. Otherwise, why would he have reported it at all? But Larkin was thorough and hated leaving anything to chance. He had requested the location of this person's chip. As long as he was anywhere aboveground, the system could locate him and check on his movements. Learning that the technician had gone to Sector 5 and was at a certain bar had turned Larkin's original conclusion on its head. That bar was well known to him because the Immaculates had watched it for weeks. They had received a tip that the TCE criminals might be using it as a meeting place. A camera was monitoring its entrance in hopes of identifying and arresting one or more of the TCE leaders.

When Larkin added up all the information, the event no longer looked innocent. The fact that the technician had gone there immediately after his experiment could only mean that he had a connection to the TCE. Possibly, he was conducting illicit experiments on their behalf. He could have logged his results to divert suspicion and make them look innocent. A team of Immaculates was immediately sent to pick him up, but instead they came back with two other men. It was maddening that he had managed to get away. His escape confirmed Larkin's suspicions, in any case.

A screen turned itself on with a beep, and the face of his head inspector appeared.

"Well? Have you got the contents of that technician's memory —what's his name, Janec?" Larkin asked.

"Nothing, sir. I'm sorry. We have analyzed the memory bank of his chip, but it seems that a large part of the location memory was canceled—a professional job. There is nothing useful there. We found only commonplace information about his workplace and home. No routing information to any other place, except, of course, for the bar where we picked him up."

"Where is he now?"

"We've put him in isolation room three."

"I'll be down in a minute. I want to talk to him. And what about the other one?"

"He was badly hurt, and I'm afraid that he won't last for long. I've connected him to a power chip to try to get whatever information he may have before he dies."

"You've done well. Keep me informed," said Larkin and switched off.

Larkin walked to the elevator that took him underground. The cells, euphemistically called "isolation rooms," were located on that level. He stopped before cell number 3 and looked at the man inside it through a one-way glass. He sat on the bench, the only piece of furniture in the room, his body strangely limp. He held his head with his hands, his body slumped as if it almost had no skeleton. The concrete walls of the room were painted bright orange. The color was meant to increase the inmate's apprehension for the future. Larkin pushed a button and spoke into the microphone of the cell's control panel. His voice boomed through the loudspeaker hidden in the ceiling, and the man jumped up in surprise.

"Janec," he said, "do you know who is speaking to you?"

"No, how could I?" Janec's tone was one of indignation. "I've been brutally attacked and brought here for no reason at all. I'm a Level Three technician, and I don't deserve such treatment. I demand to speak immediately with your superior."

"I have no superior, and I decide your fate. You are a traitor and a criminal," Larkin said calmly, "and we are treating you as such. But we will be merciful if you cooperate. We want you to lead us to the headquarters of the criminals who call themselves TCE. After you do that, we will recondition you into a useful member of society. I don't want to destroy you, but I will if I must. And if you don't cooperate, we will get to them anyway in the end. Your sacrifice will be for nothing. An easy decision, right?"

"Go to hell!" Janec said, speaking to the walls. "Go to hell," he repeated after a short silence.

"You leave me no choice," said Larkin, with a false sadness in his voice, "but to send *you* to hell. And in hell, you'll remain until you are ready to talk."

With that, he pushed a button in the panel, producing a control box. It displayed a variety of virtual-reality generation options that would be transmitted directly to the chip of the person imprisoned in room number 3. After a brief hesitation, Larkin chose one of the buttons and touched it. Then he waited for Janec to start screaming.

His jailer had stopped talking. Janec didn't know who was speaking to him, but it was clear he was of high rank. *His threats didn't work, and he's debating what to do*, he thought. *All I need to do is stay calm and refuse to talk. At some point, that will wear him out.* He went back to the bench and sat down. A scratching noise coming from a corner of the room attracted his attention. He watched in horror as a cockroach emerged from a hole in the wall, followed by another, then many more. The room was filling quickly with cockroaches. He hated cockroaches. It was the insect that he found the most disgusting. A shiver ran down his spine, and beads of perspiration appeared on his brow.

They are not real, he said to himself. *They are images, virtual reality. If I stay calm, they will go away*, he rationalized. *I need to remain seated and show them that I don't care. That's the only way I can get through this.*

But the cockroaches started climbing on his legs, and he felt his skin crawling with them. He closed his eyes and tried to imagine that the room was bare and empty as before. But the augmented reality signal was powerful, and he actually felt the insects' legs on his skin. He opened his eyes again, watched a cockroach land on the tip of his nose, and watched it start making its way into a nostril. Then he screamed.

With the last drops of rational thought left in him, Janec understood what he had to do to make it stop. He summoned all his willpower to walk to the end of the room. He needed to ignore the crisp noise of crushing the carpet of cockroaches. The insects had meanwhile covered the floor, forming a solid, pulsating layer. He turned around and ran to the other end of the room, hitting the wall with all his strength. His head hit the wall right above his ear, where the scar from the implantation of the chip was. As his body hit the ground, the control panel showed that his brain activity had stopped. He didn't hear Larkin's exclamation of dismay coming through the concealed loudspeaker.

CHAPTER 7

Kal and Amber had to go back for a good half-hour to reach the other tunnel. They reached a small passage branching off their tunnel. They hadn't noticed it before, simply because they were not looking for it. The path took them to a dead end with a vertical shaft fitted with steel stairs. It was too dark to see where the stairs led, but after a brief hesitation, they climbed them. The vertical passage ended in a small chamber with an opening into a larger one. When they switched their lamp to its highest intensity, it revealed a cavern. A ledge went from the small chamber along the cavern wall and into an opening at the other end. They studied it, and then Amber turned the light back to its minimal power.

"I don't know about you," she said, "but I'm too tired to tackle that ledge. We've been walking for almost twelve hours now. We must rest before we go on."

"I agree. That walk looks pretty scary to me, and I'm too shaky to do it right now. I'm sure it's safe to sleep a little here before we go on."

Amber untied the blanket from the top of her rucksack and laid it on the floor of the small chamber.

"Take your blanket. We'll need to stay close and well covered if we don't want to freeze in this place. It's okay when we walk, but otherwise, it's too cold."

They placed their rucksacks next to each other as pillows, and then they lay on Amber's blanket. Amber then lay down and spread Kal's blanket over them. Kal found the physical closeness to Amber embarrassing. It clashed with the education that had conditioned him to respect others' personal space. He moved to the edge of the blanket to give her more room.

"Get closer," she ordered, tugging at his sleeve. "We need to keep each other warm."

Kal's embarrassment mounted when, turning to face her, he found that Amber meant getting *really* close. She nestled her head in the hollow of his shoulder, and her body touched his along its entire length. But he had to admit that the position created a warm area that was pleasant enough to overcome his embarrassment. He remained still, unsure of what movements might seem inappropriate. He closed his eyes and tried to find sleep, but his mind had too much to process to let him.

"Are you asleep?" Amber whispered after a while.

"No. You?"

"Obviously not," she said, and her answer carried a smile at the question's stupidity. "Perhaps in a little while. I was thinking."

"Yes?"

"If you need to know, I was thinking that abandoning my mission ... makes me sad."

"What is your mission? You keep mentioning it, and I don't know what it is about."

Amber sat up, leaning against her rucksack, and Kal did the same.

"No peeping into my brain as I tell you?" she requested.

"Promise."

"I'll tell you, but it's a long story."

"I have time," said Kal, smiling.

"You should know that my father is a great scientist. He worked together with the man known as the High Professor, but that was many years ago. They were friends once. Then they disagreed on the direction in which the High Professor was steering The City. My father left The City—actually, fled it—and wound up in Freeland. There, he met my mother and settled down. You don't know a lot about Freeland, do you?"

"Actually, I know nothing. Until Seth mentioned it, I didn't know it existed."

"Freeland, as its name indicates, is a free zone. Free from the tyranny of the High Professor, I mean. As Seth told you, it is quite far from here. To get there, you must cross some wild places, which is what keeps it safe from The City. That's where my father met Afex—I'll tell you more about him in a minute. They developed much of Freeland's existing technology. Then, two years ago, the Immaculates organized a raid on Freeland and kidnapped my father. He's been a prisoner of the High Professor ever since. My mission was to rescue him from his prison."

"How awful! This must have been terrible for you."

"It was. I was only fifteen at the time and didn't know what to do. But when I turned sixteen, I decided to go to The City and find my father. Sixteen is the age of maturity in Freeland."

Kal was shocked. Amber's demeanor was that of a mature woman. Her self-assurance was remarkable, and he had come to think of her as someone of his own age.

"But that means that now you are ... barely seventeen? And what does your mother have to say about it?"

"What do you mean by 'barely'? That's my age, and I'm a grown-up. That's how it goes in Freeland. Anyway, my mother died when I was very young, and I don't remember her too well. My father is all I have ... well, besides Afex."

"I'm sorry to hear that. I grew up without my parents, but they are alive, and I get ... I got to see them now and then. Not having that must be hard."

"It was. So, I made meticulous preparations for six months before coming here. It wasn't easy, but Afex helped me when he saw that my mind was made up and that I was ready to go. Afex is my uncle, my mother's brother. He's also the chairman of the Council of Freeland, so his word counts. He's a dear, and seeing him, you wouldn't think him powerful. He's a mild man but wise and strong. So when he agreed to let me go on my rescue mission, it meant a lot to me. And now, I had to abandon the whole thing because of you."

"I'm sorry." Kal didn't know what else to say.

"It's not your fault," said Amber, in a conciliatory tone. She remained thoughtful for a few seconds, and then she continued. "You know that tattoo of mine ...."

"Yes?"

"My mother had one like it, and that's the only thing I remember well about her. I can't remember her face, but I remember that symbol. I tattooed it on my shoulder, so I have something to remember her by every day. Can you understand that? Do you think it is important enough to 'blemish' my body, as you put it?"

"I'm sorry," Kal said again, "I didn't know. Of course, it's your right, and I shouldn't be judgmental."

"You seem to be sorry a lot today," said Amber with a smile. "Well, now that I've got this off my chest, let's try to sleep some."

She slid down from her improvised pillow, and Kal did the same. This time, he turned to her and allowed her into his personal space. They huddled close together and soon fell asleep.

——— · ——— · ———

Amber woke up with a jerk. The sound she had heard could have come from the nearby cave, or she could have imagined it. She got out from under the blanket, trying not to wake Kal, shivering in the cold draft coming from the cave. The darkness was complete, and she groped for the lamp. When she found it, she turned it on at its lowest power, only enough to see where she was going. She trod gingerly on the slippery floor up to the cave's entrance. She stood there in silence and listened. All she heard was the sound of air flowing in the cave and the sporadic drip of water seeping from its ceiling. *No man-made sounds*, she concluded.

She went back inside the small chamber and looked at Kal sleeping. She was ambivalent about him. On the one hand, she was angry at him for coming uninvited to turn her life upside down. But she was fair enough and admitted to herself that it was unreasonable to blame him for it. Besides, she couldn't help feeling sorry for him. His own world has changed in a moment, through no fault of his. And she had to hand it to him that he was handling it well, everything considered. True, at first he had been a bit of a wuss, but that was understandable, given how disoriented he must have been. Once they had explained the facts to him, he had become practical and helpful.

And he is handsome, she said to herself, blushing a bit at the thought. *I hope he isn't listening in on me*, she thought. In Freeland, girls her age had already formed bonds with boys. They had to. That was the natural order of things in their liberated society. Selecting a partner for life at a young age was the norm, and marriages lasted a lifetime. Despite the free, uninhibited lifestyle of Freeland's youth, matrimony was sacred to them. When you chose a mate, you had to choose well, because it was for good.

Amber was beautiful above the norm. Even now, with her close-cut hair and ragged clothes, sweaty after a day of hard walking in a hot, damp place that had turned cold, she was undeniably attractive. Hardship seemed to bring out the best in her. Her determination radiated not only from her round face but also from every fiber of her body. That, and her social status, made her a coveted catch. But back in Freeland, she hadn't had time for that. Preparing for her expedition into The City had required all her attention, time, and strength. She had ignored insistent invitations from boys and young men, and after a while, they had given up courting her. Many had labeled her "weird" and left her alone. A couple of them had given her heart flutters, but she didn't have time for them. She was determined to embark on what Afex used to call "her mad plan." So no matter how hard they had tried to woo her, she had looked the other way and ignored them.

Uncle Afex was like a second father to her and had been her acting parent since the kidnapping of her father. He and Amber's father had been friends before her mother had come into the picture. In fact, Afex used to tell her that it was her mother who had courted her father. "You remind me very much of her. She was as hard-headed as you are," he used to say to Amber. Afex was kind and protective, but he knew her too well to think he could dissuade her from doing what she had set her heart on. When he realized that nothing he said could change her mind, he switched from trying to talk her out of it to supporting her. She missed him.

Standing there, deep in thought, Amber shivered at the cold of the chamber. She returned under the blanket, thankful for the warmth that welcomed her back. Kal stirred and opened an eye.

"Time to go?" he asked in a murmur.

"Not yet. Go on sleeping," she said.

She took one last look at Kal, then reached for the lamp and turned it off.

CHAPTER 8

"Ah, Larkin," the High Professor acknowledged his entrance.

"Alvin," Larkin started. He was one of the very few who got to call him by name. To everybody else, he was "the High Professor," but Larkin was one of his closest allies, arguably the most precious of all. His skillful control of the Immaculates and his ruthless ways had proven invaluable more than once. Larkin, for his part, enjoyed wielding the power he had and didn't mind letting Alvin play the benevolent monarch.

"Yes?"

"I've got something interesting for you. You know that chipless savage that we took into custody in that bar? His name was Jamie."

"You mentioned a chipless individual. What about him?"

"When they brought him here, he was already almost dead. I'm glad that they didn't finish him there because I was able to get an interesting piece of information from him that may turn out to be quite valuable."

"You said that he was almost dead already," said Alvin, "so how did you—"

"I plugged one of those high-power chips into his brain and connected him to a reader. I recorded a lot of information about the last few weeks, including some good images. So it turns out that he was intimate with a chipless savage by the name of Amber. She escaped our raid, and we don't know where she is, but we know *who* she is."

"Who is she?"

"Believe it or not, she's Sazar's daughter," Larkin said triumphantly.

"Really? And what is she doing here?" Alvin raised an eyebrow. That information seemed too far-fetched to be true.

"I gather that she has some silly notion of rescuing her father from his prison."

"How sure are you that this information is reliable? It sounds too fantastic to be true."

"I told you that I managed to get some good material, and that includes a mental image of the girl. Look at it," he added, pointing his control device to the large screen on the wall.

The screen lit up, and then an image of a young girl appeared. Alvin scrutinized the image on the screen.

"The resemblance is striking, I admit. She looks like him. Yes, you must be right."

"I am right. And there is something else that you may be able to explain. Look at this other picture. It's a detail of the girl's shoulder. Do you see those signs there? That's a tattoo of a sun in a circle. Does that mean anything to you?"

"No. I've never seen a symbol like that before."

"Well, anyway, it will help us to identify her."

"We must find her. You said that she got away?"

"Yes. We don't know where she is. I tried to get more information from this Jamie individual, but I couldn't find anything more useful before he died. If she's here on a mission to rescue her father, she must be hiding somewhere with the TCE crew. That means that we must go light on them to avoid killing her. We need her alive to force Sazar to do his part."

"But she could have run away from The City if she got scared enough after the raid. You know that there are still many tunnels connecting The City with the outside."

"I know. We work hard to find and seal them, but there are too many, and some are hard to find. Anyway, I'll put out a call for her capture with a nice reward. The savages who live around The City will run to us with her if they find her in one of their territories."

"You do that. Meanwhile, I'll start using this piece of information. What's the girl's name, again?"

"Amber."

Sazar's "prison" was a comfortable one. In fact, in the quarters assigned to him in a wing of the High Professor's headquarters, he spent his days reading. His apartment was spacious, with a living room adjoining a bedroom with a private bath. He was only allowed out in the headquarters' inner yard for airings every other day, and then he was carefully guarded. Even now, two Immaculates stood guard outside his room.

Alvin found him gazing out the window at the complex's inner garden.

"How are you today, Sazar?" he asked with fake comradeship.

Sazar turned without haste to face him and remained silent.

"I'm truly interested in your welfare, my friend—"

"We are not friends!" Sazar interrupted him.

"Shall I say 'former friend,' then?" said Alvin with a bitter smile.

"Say whatever you like. I don't care."

"Listen, why can't you be reasonable? We used to work so well together. All I need from you is a little help, and then I'll have you returned to your home. I can't understand why you are so stubborn. After all, we were working on it together. We were a team. Don't I have any rights to the result of this work?"

Alvin heated up as he always did when talking to Sazar, who remained frosty and quiet.

"We've been through this a hundred times. What you want to do will turn everyone with a chip into a marionette, even more than they are today. When we started this work, following that of our mentor, the first High Professor, we wanted to do good. We aimed to shelter our people from the plagues of the world outside, to give them a healthy, good life. And look what you've done with that—you have taken their freedom away by feeding their brains with lies! If I were to tell you how to change their memories as well, I would become a criminal just like you. I won't do it."

"You know that I am doing good to our people. You understand that the world outside has regressed by five hundred years. The environmental damage, the lack of technology, and the diseases exist everywhere but in The City. Look what we have accomplished here. There is no one else who can give hope to our people for a better future!"

Alvin started to get excited, as he always did when talking about his perceived accomplishments.

"That's not true. There are many good places to live, like Freeland."

"Freeland, tcha! Freeland will soon become one of The City's provinces. I told you about New City—the city we started building at the edge of the territories you call Freeland. It is a matter of time before we use our superior technology to seize power there. You could prevent all that if you only worked with me. My offer to make you the High Professor of New City and rule it for me is still standing. Help me, and you'll have a position fit for your ability."

"Why can't you leave Freeland alone? They are much more advanced than you think, and seizing power there will be a tall order. You'll find out soon enough if you dare attack Freeland. You're inviting a bloodbath, and for the sake of what? Your ego?"

"My ego has nothing to do with this. I haven't told you before, but I'll tell you now. The City is dying. We have no natural resources. We're living on recycled resources from the old days, with the addition of a little import from the Surroundings. It's getting harder day by day, and in ten years, people here will start to starve. We have no choice but to make a fresh start somewhere with resources, far from the epicenter of The Pulse. That's Freeland, and we are going to do it. It's my responsibility."

"Instead of your plans of aggression, you could negotiate a pact with Freeland to the benefit of us both."

"That's not an option. I heard your foolish ideas—that we go back to the old ways and stop regulating people's lives with the chip. That's never going to happen, so you may as well make peace with it and start cooperating."

Sazar ostentatiously turned his back to him and gazed outside again. Alvin's face reddened, and he grabbed his arm.

"Look here," he said, speaking furiously, "I don't know why I don't let Larkin plug one of his high-powered chips into your head and suck all the information from your brain."

"I know why. You understand as well as I do that you won't be able to get the information you want. You don't dare risk ruining my brain forever. Perhaps you should do it and get it over with. Better than remaining a prisoner here. Life here has no meaning to me, and I don't care anymore if I live or die."

"I believe you, but maybe you will care about the welfare of your daughter ...."

"What are you talking about?"

"I didn't know that you had a daughter, but I do now."

"So?"

"So, you wouldn't want anything unpleasant to happen to her, I presume."

"She's far away and safe from you, and I don't believe that you know anything about her beyond your wild guess that I have one."

"Her name is Amber, isn't it? She looks very much like you," Alvin said with a smirk. He displayed a large, bright photograph on the tablet he was carrying.

"Where did you get that picture?"

"From someone here in The City. That's how we know she's here."

"I don't believe you."

"You'd better believe me. It appears that she has some foolish romantic idea about rescuing you, as if that were possible. If you give me what I need, we will announce your release and departure for Freeland immediately. Once you are safe, she won't attempt anything stupid. She's chipless like you and me, right? And you know what happens to chipless criminals if they run into an Immaculate patrol. Of course, we'd prefer to capture her alive, but mistakes occur."

"You make sure that no mistakes occur with her," said Sazar. "Because if anything happens to her, you will never, ever get what you want from me."

"I'll leave you alone to think about this. I'm sure you'll know what you have to do."

Yes, Sazar thought, *I know. When I'm dead, and he can no longer blackmail me, Alvin will have no use for Amber, and she will be safe.*

He touched his upper left molar with his finger as if to make sure that it was still there. It had been many years since he had thought about the poison capsule hidden in his artificial tooth. He had it installed many years back when planning the failed coup to oust Alvin from power after learning of the mental tortures used by his minions to extort information from captured plotters. Many had betrayed other members of the network, but he would never be a traitor. He had never needed to use it but had kept it there just in case, and was now happy to have it. To release the poison, he had to unscrew the false molar, retrieve a sealed glass ampulla, and crush it between his teeth. He knew that the poison was not a very strong one, so, to ensure death, he needed to ingest it to the last drop. The surveillance cameras that monitored his every movement would make it difficult to use it, but he would find the right moment. He was determined and entirely at peace with his decision.

CHAPTER 9

"Take off your clothes," Amber said.

"What?" Kal sounded astonished.

They had finally woken up, somewhat rested by an uncomfortable sleep. They ate some more bread and cheese and then braved the walk along the cavern ledge. They had to go through more narrow passages before they reached the underground river. That meant that they were close to the alternative tunnel and to the surface. But they had to cross that river first. It was not very wide—about fifty feet—and not very deep, either. Using her stick, Amber had estimated the depth to be waist height. But the water was freezing.

"You heard me. If you go into the river with your clothes on, you'll get to the other side completely drenched. And if you plan to walk around with wet clothing, I guarantee that you'll get pneumonia in no time and die. I don't think that your sheltered life as a bubble boy has prepared you for this. It wouldn't be healthy for me, either, despite my outdoor upbringing. But if you pack your clothes in the rucksack, which is waterproof, you'll keep them dry. Once you get to the other side, you'll dry yourself off with your blanket before dressing up again. That means you'll be cold for only a short time and will end up dressed again in dry clothes. Which way makes the most sense to you?"

"Yes, but—"

"But what?"

"There has to be another way to do it. To be honest, I am uncomfortable with this. Undressing in front of someone else, and a girl of all people ... this is not how I was educated."

"You were also educated to think that the world is beautiful and the High Professor is your friend. Forget what you have learned. You're no longer a City man. You're a fugitive, a pariah, and you must behave like one. So now listen: you do it your way, and I'll do it my way. I'm not going to catch pneumonia, and I'm not staying here."

With those words, Amber started to undress. She took off her shoes and unbuttoned her shirt. Kal turned his back to her, uncomfortable at the mere thought that she was stripping. He listened to the sounds of her movements as she undressed and prepared to cross. Then he heard the splashing of her wading through the water. He waited, unsure what to do next.

"I've arrived. I'm covered; you can turn around," she called from the other side after a while. "I'll turn my back to you, and you can undress and cross as I did. I promise not to peek."

There was little else that Kal could do. In the end, he was a rational person. He stripped, stuffed his clothes into the water-proof rucksack, and stepped into the water.

"I'm coming," he called out.

"Not looking," came the reply.

The water was freezing, and Kal waded as fast as he could. He kept the rucksack above his head and well away from the water. At first, the crossing went well, but as he approached the other bank, his legs began to feel numb from the cold, and that's when he made a false move. He had stepped on a round, slippery rock and realized that he had lost his balance and was about to go down. With an effort, he threw his rucksack as far away as he could. He heard it land on dry ground, but that movement made him lose the little balance he still had.

"Ah!" he cried, splashing into the icy water.

The current was not very fast, but it was enough to carry him away from his crossing point and over a bend. He lost sight of the little light Amber's lamp cast near the crossing. Kal's senses were so confused by the darkness and the cold that for a moment, he didn't know which way to turn. He tried to fight the current that was pulling him away, but he began to lose feeling in his limbs. He heard Amber calling his name, and that helped him regain some orientation. He threw his arms out, looking for something to hold on to. His hand finally met a rocky formation, which he grabbed. With his remaining strength, he pulled himself onto the riverbank and lay there, frozen and unable to move or speak, shivering from the cold. He lost track of time. As he fought to stay conscious, his eyes caught sight of a distant light that seemed to be moving toward him. It was far away, and he tried to follow it, but then he passed out.

In his confusion, he wasn't sure if what he heard was a voice or a thought.

"You'll be all right."

To Kal, Amber's voice seemed to come from a distance. He felt a blanket thrown onto him. He opened his eyes and realized that she was above him and was massaging his body so hard that it hurt.

"Get up. You need to move and to get your blood circulation to work," she said without stopping.

Kal nodded, too weak to speak. Amber's hands on him felt like fire running over his body wherever she touched him. Still, he didn't want it to stop because his body felt numb again when she moved to a different place. He irrationally feared that he would freeze solid if she stopped doing that. Amber grabbed him under his armpit and encouraged him to stand up, which he did with difficulty. As soon as he assumed a standing position, she wrapped the blanket all around him and kept massaging him.

"It's okay now," he said feebly when he started to feel his body again. "Thank you. You're a savior."

"I'm sorry that it took me a long time to find you. This place is dark, and my light is weakening. Can you walk? We need to go back to our rucksacks and get your clothes."

"I think so," said Kal.

He started to walk but had to stop after a second.

"Don't be a hero," she said. "Here, lean on me."

Slowly and cautiously, they made their way back to their rucksacks.

"Are you up to dressing?" she asked when they got there.

"Yes, I'm fine now. Thanks to you," he said. He breathed heavily and shivered.

"You don't look fine to me. Don't overdo it. I can help you get dressed. It's no big deal ... I've already seen you naked anyway," she added with a smile.

"Thank you, but I'll manage," Kal said. He hoped that the bad lighting was hiding his blush.

"Good. Good," she said, and then she turned around to let him have some privacy.

59

CHAPTER 10

As soon as Kal felt strong enough, they followed the route traced on the map. They walked through another tunnel before turning toward what they hoped would be their exit. Every few minutes, they had to stop to rest because Kal was dizzy and weak. When he was too tired to go on, they slept for a couple of hours and then kept going. They walked in silence for more than three hours. At first, Kal tried to walk at a normal pace, but his gait kept slowing over time. He was having trouble breathing, and, despite his efforts to hide it, it was clear that something was wrong with him. The cavernous cough that came from him now and then was troubling.

Finally, seeing the light at the end of the tunnel had lifted a heavy burden off their shoulders—the exit was open. At last, they emerged from it. Kal gaped at the scenery for a long minute, transfixed by the novel sensation of being out there in the open. The entrance to the tunnel was behind a hill that hid it from sight. Majestic trees and abundant mixed vegetation covered the top of the hill. Kal stood, transfixed by the beauty of it all. His eyes couldn't let go of two colorful butterflies fluttering nearby. Amber had to nudge him to move on. Slowly, with Amber adjusting to

Kal's hesitant pace, they climbed to the top of the hill. The day was beautiful, with a bright sun, a cool breeze, and even a bird of sorts circling above them in the sky. In the distance, more trees and green grass covered the earth as far as Kal's eyes reached. Amber dropped her rucksack and then threw herself onto the grass.

"God! Seeing the light of day again is awesome!"

"So this is what being outside feels like," Kal murmured in awe. The beauty of the countryside was such that, for a moment, he forgot how bad he felt.

"Come, sit here," Amber ordered, and Kal dropped onto the grass beside her.

He turned his gaze hungrily all around him, shading his eyes from the strong sunlight with his hand. His expression was serious.

"What's the matter?" she asked. "You should be happy that we finally got out, so why the long face?"

"I'm sorry, you're right. I'm not myself. I feel ... I feel strange. I've never felt this way."

Amber was worried. Kal's eyes were watery, and beads of perspiration had appeared on his brow. She gently touched his cheek with her hand.

"Shit! You have a fever. You're hot."

"A fever? I've never had a fever before. Is this how it feels?"

"You tell me that you've never been sick before? Are you kidding me? I've got the fever a million times."

"My H-cubicle always took care of my health. I've never had to worry about it."

"Well, there's no H-cubicle or any other fancy City equipment here. But the good news is that you'll be able to rest and get medical care where we are going. We need to reach our first stop as soon as possible and find you some good medicines."

"The way I feel, I'm not sure that I can walk for long ...."

"It's not far from here. We can make it in an hour. I'll help you."

Amber got up and gave him a hand, helping him to his feet.

"It's lucky that you are skinny," she said, smiling.

Kal smiled back, but it was a weary smile.

"All right," said Amber, eyeing him and grimacing. "You're in no shape to carry that rucksack another yard. Give it to me."

"No, I'm okay! You can't carry my load for me. I can do it. Just help me to get it up on my shoulders."

Amber realized that carrying both their rucksacks would be too much for her. She debated whether to leave it there and come to pick it up later. After a moment, she decided that they should try to make it with all their belongings. Without speaking, she helped Kal shoulder his rucksack. Then, slowly, they started down the hill.

They had been walking at a slow pace—one that was maddening to Amber—, and it took them the best part of two hours to reach C-54. The travel lodge was a strange building built around a cubic concrete body. It was obviously ancient, and a second floor made of wood, assorted metal sheets, and clay was patched on top of it. It stood on flat ground against the backdrop of distant, green hills. It was an ugly building. Someone had tried to hide its ugliness by growing a few decorative cacti next to its facade, but that didn't help much. Still, to Amber, tired as she was, it was a beautiful vision.

Nobody knew the origin of the building's name. Its story went back to a military station of unknown purpose and origin. It was a convenient place to stop when traveling from north to south at the edge of the Surroundings. That area was a narrow strip of land between The City and the LAP land—an acronym for "Left After The Pulse." It was a wild, almost lawless, vast land, where survivors of The Pulse had begun a new life amid the ruins of the old civilization. An old couple ran the travel lodge. Amber had stopped there for a few days before entering the tunnel that got her into The City. The owner, Adam, was a friend of Afex's, and he seemed to know everybody everywhere. He had helped her with food and equipment.

Kal had reached the point where he could barely drag his feet as he walked, leaning on Amber, his eyes cloudy.

A man whom Amber immediately recognized as Adam emerged from the building and waved at them from afar.

"Good God! What happened to you? And who's this?" he cried when they got close enough to hear.

Adam ran up to them and relieved Amber of the weight of Kal's body. He was about seventy (Amber never asked him his actual age), but still strong. His white hair and beard made you feel you were in the presence of wisdom, inner peace, and strength. So did his usually slow, precise manner of speech. He could be counted on in an emergency.

"I'll explain later," she said. "He's sick. He's got a fever and needs help."

"Let's get him inside, and I'll have Sarah take a look at him."

Sarah, Adam's wife, was the life and spirit of the travel lodge. She cooked, cleaned, and doubled as a doctor in times of need. As far as Amber knew, she didn't have formal medical training, but she had acquired experience by treating many people over the years. She had taken care of a blister on the sole of Amber's foot the first time she had stayed at the travel lodge on her way to The City. "Lucky we got it in time before it became infected," she had said. It had hurt so much that it was a surprise it wasn't already infected. With Sarah's ointment, Amber was ready to walk again in no time.

They helped Kal inside, with Adam taking most of his weight. Amber was already exhausted from assisting Kal to walk all the way, and now that he wasn't helping at all, he was definitely too heavy for her. Adam piloted them to the first room in a row, and together they laid him on the bed.

"Sarah!" Adam bellowed, and an old woman with a round, smiling face walked into the room.

"No need to shout, dear husband. It is you who's half deaf, not me. Oh, it's you, sweetie! Great surprise! Good to see you back in one piece," she added, seeing Amber. She kissed her on the cheek and then noticed Kal lying on the bed. "What do we have here?" she inquired.

"This is my friend, Kal. He isn't well. He needs help."

Right then, Amber decided not to tell them who Kal was and what they were planning. Too dangerous to even say the words. It wasn't that she didn't trust them; she did. But Kal was too important to endanger him in any way.

"He's unconscious. What happened to him?"

"We were coming here through one of the tunnels, and we had to cross an underground river. He fell into freezing water."

"He's a city boy, isn't he?"

Despite the tension and fatigue, Amber smiled to herself. It was funny, she thought, to refer to a physicist who could hold the key to the end of tyranny and to a brand-new world as a "boy." But then, from the perspective of her sixty-something years, everybody would look young to Sarah.

"Yes," Amber conceded, "he grew up in The City."

"Then he's in trouble. I've had to treat city people before, and their immune systems are a wreck. They grow up in a bubble and may die if you sneeze on them. I'll see what I can do, but he's in bad shape, and I don't know if he can take the treatment that I need to give him. Oh, well, we'll see."

"Please, Sarah," Amber pleaded. She felt a lump in her throat. If asked only a day before, she would have said that Kal's fate was of no concern to her. But something had changed during their time together in that dark tunnel.

"Of course, I'll do my best, my dear. I always do. But sometimes my best is not good enough. Now get out of here and let me take care of him."

"Don't you need help? I can help."

"The shape you're in now, I doubt you can help yourself. Adam, take her to a room and get her some food. You need to eat and rest. Now go away, both of you, and let me work," she added, and then she turned her back to Amber and placed her ear to Kal's chest.

When Amber woke up, it was already dark. The air in the room was stuffy, and she was sweaty. Much against her will, she had allowed Sarah to convince her to get some sleep. Despite the turmoil of her thoughts, she had fallen asleep almost immediately. Sarah had ruled that Amber would be of no help in treating Kal and would only be in the way. So, after a quick but satisfying meal, she had taken a room near Kal's, closed the shutters, and crashed on the bed.

She got up and walked to the nearby bathroom with heavy feet. She splashed cold water on her face, and then she went to look for her hosts. She found them at the kitchen table, talking.

"Oh, you're up. Good," said Adam.

"How's Kal?" Amber asked.

"Asleep. I gave him something to help him sleep. He needs it more than anything else," said Sarah.

"Yes, but how is he doing?"

"Too early to say. I did all I could to help him, but now it's up to him. Let's hope that his immune system is equal to the task. It's amazing how quickly he worked up a fever."

"I want to see him," said Amber, and Sarah got up without arguing and led the way.

In the semi-dark room, Amber stooped over the bed. She watched Kal until she was sure he was, in fact, breathing. He breathed so shallowly that at times she wasn't sure. He didn't seem to be in pain but looked kind of lifeless. She touched his forehead.

"He's still hot and is sweating," she said.

"I've given him something to lower his temperature, but I can't give him too much. He's not used to drugs, and an overdose may do him more harm than help."

"I'll sit here with him," said Amber.

"No, you won't. It wouldn't do him any good. Or you. Let's go back to the kitchen. Adam has made coffee."

In the kitchen, Amber sat with them at the table and forced herself to be practical.

"I need to get in touch with Afex, Adam. He has to send an aerial platform to pick us up. Can you call him for me?"

"Oh my," said Adam, shaking his head. "My radio—the one I use to speak with the outside world—is out of order. Last week, I ordered a replacement for the faulty part from someone who was passing through here. He's due to come back in a few days. I think that he should be here in two or three days, but until then, I'm afraid that I have no way to make contact."

"Your friend is in no shape to travel anyway and won't be for at least a day or two—if everything goes well," said Sarah. "I'm afraid that you'll have to suffer the company of us old folks for a little longer," she added, smiling.

"You know that I love being here with you," said Amber. "It's just that I'm worried about Kal. Perhaps if I could get him to a hospital in Freeland, that might make a difference."

"I doubt it. It's pretty much up to his body whether it can fight the infection. Medical intervention can only help so much."

"It's not that I don't trust you; you know that I do. But how can you be sure that we aren't missing something important?"

"I haven't always been a hermit, you know. Before my dear husband kidnapped me to this godforsaken place, I was an assistant to a gifted healer. I saw and helped him treat more cases than you can count for ten years, and he taught me all he knew. I can't make miracles, but I know what I'm doing."

"You stop worrying your pretty head," said Adam. "Sarah

never wants to take credit for anything, bless her soul. But she does marvels with her herbs and potions, and I'm sure that your boy will be fine. Now you go and get a good night's sleep, and let us do the same. Sarah and I will take turns checking on him, and if we need you, we'll wake you up."

"Thank you, Adam. Thank you, Sarah. I can't tell you how much I appreciate all you're doing."

"Don't mention it," said Adam, making a dismissive gesture. "Afex is family, and so are you. Good night."

"Good night," said Amber.

On her way to her room, she stopped by Kal's bed again. He hadn't moved at all since her last visit. He looked so young and vulnerable that she couldn't keep a tear of helplessness from rolling down her cheek. She turned and almost fled from the room. She couldn't bear to see him like that.

CHAPTER 11

"Someone in there."

"Is he dead?"

"No, but look at him. He's sick."

"You're right. He may be contagious. Let's get the hell outta here."

Sounds of voices and shouting, doors slamming, and more voices. Loud voices. All fought for Kal's attention, but only managed to reach him for a few seconds. Then he drifted away again into a dreamless sleep.

The day turned into night and then back into day. Kal's throat burned with thirst, but the fever was gone, and he felt consciousness coming back to him. He opened his eyes and blinked against the bright light. He struggled to remember where he was and how he had gotten there. He was nauseous, his mouth was pasty, and his head hurt. He tried to sit up, but that only brought black spots before his eyes.

Someone was in the room with him. An old woman. Her face was vaguely familiar; he knew he had seen her before, but she was different now. She had clotted blood on the side of her face where her hair seemed to be missing. She was sitting beside him, saying something. Kal made an effort to concentrate and listen to her.

"Can you hear me?" she said. She spoke in a hoarse, low voice, and speaking was obviously an effort to her.

"Where am I? Who are you?" Kal asked at last.

"Don't you remember anything? Amber brought you here four days ago. You had a fever and were delirious. I took care of you. The fever is gone now."

"Amber? Where is she?"

"They took her. I'll tell you everything. Drink this first."

She was handing him a cup, and Kal drank it. The liquid had a foul taste and stung his tongue. Still, his throat was sore, like sandpaper, and the liquid helped a little, so he drank it. He finished all the liquid in the cup and handed it back to the woman.

"I'm Sarah," she said.

"Sarah—I heard that name. Yes, I remember. Where is Amber?"

"I don't know. The people—those who came yesterday—they took her away, after ... after ...."

"What people. What are you saying? You are hurt!" he exclaimed, becoming aware that she wasn't well.

His senses were coming back to him, and his vision grew clearer.

"They came yesterday and ransacked our place. They took everything we had, and they took Amber. They left me for dead, or I wouldn't be here to tell you about it. You were in terrible shape, so I guess they didn't bother with you. They left you here to die."

Kal sat up, looking the woman in the eyes. He felt a little stronger now and more capable of understanding what she was saying. She, in contrast, was clearly in bad shape. She had dragged a chair next to his bed and was sitting with her upper body bent forward. Besides the blood on the side of her head, her left arm hung at an awkward angle, and she held it with her right hand.

"But that's terrible. You need help. Tell me how I can help you."

"There isn't much that you can do for me. I gave myself a shot, and I'm not hurting too much, but I don't think that I'll hold on for long. You must help me to bury Adam."

"Who's Adam?"

"My husband. He's the one who brought you in. They shot him at the door, and he's been there since. I can't leave him there, and I don't have the strength to carry him myself and bury him. I need your help."

She spoke in a matter-of-fact manner that sent a chilling shiver down Kal's spine. He didn't know what to say.

"I'm sorry," he finally managed to articulate.

"I never imagined that it would end like this. Adam never hurt a fly. He was the gentlest soul and my soulmate for … so many years, but now—" Sarah wiped her eyes with her good hand. It wiped a solitary tear as if that one tear was all she had left after already crying her fill. She paused for a moment, then continued speaking. Her monotonous voice seemed designed to keep emotion away.

"Don't worry about that, now," she said. "The drink that I gave you should give you enough energy to get up and help me. There's a bit more left in that bottle over there, and you'll need it when you leave here. The fever is gone, but you'll be weak for another few days. The energy drink will help you."

"I'm not going anywhere," Kal protested. "You need help, and I won't leave you. You looked after me, and now I'll look after you."

"You have to go," she said patiently. "They haven't taken all our supplies—it was too much for them to carry. They will be back for the rest, and when they come, you can't be here, or they'll kill you."

"Then you have to come with me!" said Kal.

Sarah gazed at him with a sad smile for a second. "I'll stay here with Adam," she said.

There was nothing more to say. Kal got gingerly to his feet and, to his surprise, found his balance again. He gave her his hand, helped her up, and together they walked along the corridor to the entrance. Adam's body almost blocked the door, and a faint smell of death reached Kal's nostrils. Kal had never smelled it before, but his instinct told him immediately what it was.

"There is a shovel in that closet over there," said Sarah, "and you'll find a stretcher there as well. Bring a wheelbarrow. We need it to carry Adam."

Kal brought the stretcher, and with the little help that Sarah could give him, they managed to put Adam's body on it. Kal tried not to look at him but couldn't help seeing the gaping hole in his chest. Once the body was on the stretcher, Kal rolled the wheelbarrow down two steps to the ground outside. Then he slid the stretcher onto it until its middle part reached its center. From that point, moving the body was easier.

Sarah led the way around the building. In the backyard, a little cemetery contained five or six marked graves. He had never been to a cemetery before, and the place looked strangely peaceful to him. There were no funerals in The City, only brief farewells. Then the Department of Family Affairs took care of the bodies.

He wasn't sure what to do next, so he followed Sarah to a corner.

"We prepared this place for us, but we thought that we wouldn't need it for a long time," she said. "Here, lift this plate. The graves are ready."

Kal lifted a sheet of corrugated metal, uncovering two twin pits. Sarah pointed at the left one, and Kal pushed the stretcher into it, unloading Adam's body as gently as he could. From the wheelbarrow, he took the shovel and stuck it into the little heap of earth beside the grave.

"In a minute," Sarah said without looking at him. She sat at the edge of the pit with her feet dangling inside.

Kal understood and walked to the other end of the cemetery to give her privacy. He waited, his back to Sarah, until she called to him.

"Now you can cover him," she said. She wiped tears from her eyes and watched in silence as Kal filled the grave. He shoveled earth until a little mound formed above the pit, and then, exhausted, he dropped the shovel.

"What now?" he asked.

"Now we go back to the house. You must eat something, and I'll get you some medical and food supplies; then you need to go. They may be back any time now."

"But where did they go? I need to find Amber."

"Don't be foolish. Those murderers kidnapped her. If you go after them, they will kill you, too. She's beyond help."

"I don't care. I can't leave her like this and run away."

"Suit yourself," she said, "but you're being a fool."

"Tell me where to find them. I'll be careful, I promise."

"I'm not sure, but I believe that I recognized one of the men. If I'm right, he comes from Komsk, a settlement about twenty miles from here. If you take the old road that goes by those trees," she added, pointing in their direction, "you'll get there. But I wouldn't travel the road in plain sight if I were you. You can follow the track that runs beside it. It is hidden from the road for much of the distance. That's the best advice that I can give you if you are stubborn and want to go and get yourself killed."

"Thank you, Sarah. I can't tell you how grateful I am for your help. Once I find Amber, I'll come back here and tell you. Meanwhile, I hope you'll manage all by yourself."

"Sure. Here's a sack with your supplies. Drink your soup and eat everything that's on that plate. And take these," she added.

"What's that?"

"Money. Silver and gold coins. It's not a lot, but it's something that Adam and I have been saving. Lucky that those bastards didn't find it."

"I can't take your money," Kal protested.

"How far do you think you can go without any money? Take it."

"You're right. I'll need some money, but I can't take it all. You may need it."

"Take it," Sarah repeated, handing it to him.

"Okay, thanks," said Kal after a brief hesitation. "I'll pay you back, I promise."

"No problem. Now get ready. I'll go and sit a little longer with Adam. Come and say goodbye before you leave."

The food was what Kal had needed to feel strong again, and he ate hungrily. He was in a hurry to start on his way and to find Amber. He still worried that Sarah would not be able to handle herself, hurt as she was, but there was little he could do about it. And if she was right that the people who had attacked them would be back, he wondered what she would do then.

Kal took the sack that Sarah had prepared for him and strode to the cemetery. She was nowhere in sight, and as he approached, he scanned the area, wondering what could have become of her. He didn't want to leave without saying goodbye, but it was getting late, and he had to get going. As he reached Adam's grave, a startling sight met his eyes. Sarah lay on her back in the open pit beside Adam's grave. Her eyes were wide open, and her good hand held an empty flask. She wasn't breathing. She had decided to stay with Adam on her own terms, and all that was left for Kal to do was cover her body.

He had never felt as sad as he did when he turned his back on the two fresh graves he had covered. With determined steps, he walked toward the old road and the unknown.

CHAPTER 12

Amber listened to the sounds outside, trying to guess what was going on. There were noises of horses and carriages and indistinct voices speaking from a distance. The barn in which they had imprisoned her was smelly, but not entirely in a bad way. At night, out of sheer exhaustion, she had managed to sleep a little on a bed of straw. Although her captors had untied her before locking her in, her wrists still hurt from the coarse rope that had tied her during the trip there.

The little light that came through gaps in the wooden wall slabs was enough for her to see the barn's interior. She was not the only one there. In the other corner, a woman lay on a few blankets and looked asleep. Amber debated whether to wake her up and talk to her. While she was trying to decide what to do, the woman stirred and sat up.

"Who are you?" she asked, eyeing her with suspicion.

"I'm Amber. You?"

"I'm Marion. Where did they get you?"

"I was at C-54—do you know where that is?"

"Yes. I know the folks there. What happened?"

"They came while we were eating. They killed Adam, and I

think they killed Sarah, too. She was in another room, and I didn't see it, but those animals joked about it. They turned the place upside down and took me."

For some reason, Amber didn't feel it was a good idea to mention Kal. She didn't know what had happened to him, but she had heard one of the men saying, "Don't go into that room. There's one in a coma there. He looks bad and may be infectious. Better not touch him," so she hoped he was unscathed. Sarah had said that he was past his crisis, and the fever was gone, so perhaps he would get out of there alive. What would he do then, though, besides getting lost? He didn't know the way to Freeland.

"Oh, poor folks! I knew them well. I grew up not far from there."

"How do you happen to be here? How old are you? How long have you been here?"

"Lots of questions," Marion said, smiling for the first time. "I'm twenty years old. I am supposed to get married a week from today. I ran away three days ago because they were forcing me to marry this old man, and I didn't want to. I have been speaking with somebody else I met at a fair, but secretly, because my family wouldn't have approved. I got here, thinking that I would pay my way east by working here and there, and that I would be safe once I got to his town. I didn't know that my future husband had put out a reward for my capture. As soon as I got here, they imprisoned me, and now I'm waiting for him to come and take me back."

"Where is 'here'?"

"This is Komsk. Don't you know anything?"

"No, I come from far away, and I don't know the area."

"Well, Komsk used to be a fracking site. They get oil for running machinery by breaking rocks. But the supply is dwindling, and most people who worked in fracking have left. They still do a little of that, but not much. Five years ago, Komsk was taken over by what they call 'a corporation.' Word is that they are bad elements and that they answer to someone named 'Chief Executive.' That's all I know."

Right then, a noise at the door announced the arrival of visitors. The door opened, and Amber squinted against the intense light from outside. Two men waited by the door, and a third came inside and stood before her. She got up and faced him. He was the leader of the men who had captured her. They hadn't spoken to her on the way to Komsk, and then they had simply thrown her into the barn. The music and laughter from afar left no doubt that they were celebrating their spoils. The man was dirty, and his breath was heavy with alcohol.

"So," he said with a smirk, "what do we have here?"

Amber stood, meeting his gaze, and did not speak.

"Where are you from, girl?" he said.

Amber kept silent; a few seconds later, a blow to the side of her face brought her to her knees.

"When I ask questions, you will answer," the man said viciously. "Where are you from?"

Amber got to her feet, trying to ignore the burning feeling on her cheek.

"Up north," she hissed.

"Name?"

"Amber. Why did you have to kill those nice old people?"

She was now trembling, but with fury, not with fear.

"They got in the way," he said dismissively. "They should have known better, and then perhaps they would still be alive. You don't get to ask questions!" he shouted in sudden anger. "Our Chief will be back tomorrow night, and then we'll decide what to do with you. We may sell you to someone in The City, or we may keep you as our slave. We can use a juicy young body like yours. The Chief will decide," he said.

He grabbed her arm and squeezed it as if to emphasize his statement. Amber pulled hard, and he opened his hand, letting her fall back onto the straw. With a loud laugh, he turned away.

"Here, we've brought you grub. We don't want you to starve. You're too precious," he said.

The two men who had waited by the door walked in with two bowls. They placed them on the floor and left, locking the door behind them.

"Animals!" Amber said, letting out her anger. "And they treat us like animals."

"You're right, but we may as well eat something," Marion said. "I haven't had anything to eat since yesterday."

Amber nodded and pulled the bowl toward her. It contained soup with a bit of meat and a potato floating in it. It smelled stale, but she was too hungry to worry about it. She ate in silence and then went back to the straw and lay there, thinking about Sarah and Adam. She had to repress her tears after remembering how she had last seen them. She had to be strong. She wouldn't let her sorry condition break her. She had to believe that Kal had survived and that he would get away safely. If he did and got to Freeland, she didn't care what happened to her. She closed her eyes and imagined a different reality, one in which he and Kal had flown to Freeland. Somehow, that restored her courage to face what would come in the days to come.

CHAPTER 13

Komsk's trading post was a building at the edge of the small town. People from all over the territory came there to buy and sell, and to merrymake at one of the local restaurants or bars. When Kal walked into the main room of the trading post, the place was crowded. Only two people manned a long counter. One was busy arguing with a stout man about a heap of plastic bags with dubious contents. The other was watching them argue. At one end of the counter, another man served drinks. A line of people waiting for the argument to end was becoming impatient. Shouts of "Get on with it!" erupted from it more and more frequently. Kal touched the shoulder of one of the men waiting in line, and he turned around.

"Yes?" he inquired.

"Pardon me. I'm new here. What's all the commotion about?" Kal asked.

"Trading day. Every month, we come to Komsk from all areas to sell and trade our merchandise. It's a crazy day. I've been waiting for an hour. I sell men's clothing, by the way. You look like you need some. Want to see?"

"No, thanks. I'm good."

"No, you aren't. Those are city clothes that you're wearing. They make you conspicuous. I don't know whether you're a deserter or a criminal, and I don't care, but I wouldn't walk around in those if I were you. City people are not welcome here. Come, my carriage is nearby. I'll fix you up in no time," he added when he saw that Kal was hesitating. "You'll feel better after you change."

"Thanks," said Kal, finally recognizing the truth of what the man said.

"I'm Abe, by the way," said the man, putting out a hand for Kal to shake. "Follow me."

The shirt and trousers that Abe offered Kal were rough to the touch, compared with the flimsy fabric of his technician's uniform. Still, they were warmer and more colorful. Moreover, wearing them meant blending with the people around him.

"You also need new boots," said Abe. "You look funny in your low shoes. My sister-in-law sells great boots. Wait here, and I'll get you a pair. I can take your shoes as part of the payment."

Abe returned with boots that Kal found immediately comfortable.

"I like them, but I don't have much money, and I'm not sure that I can afford them," he said.

A lengthy negotiation followed. Abe offered to accept Kal's uniform as partial payment, but Kal declined. He didn't know when he might need it again. After a heated back-and-forth, Kal parted with two pieces of silver and one of gold. He wasn't sure that it was a good bargain, but it was almost half the price that Abe had demanded to begin with.

Dressed in local clothing, Kal walked into the trading post again. He tried to open his mind to the thoughts of those around him, but the sheer number of thoughts almost blinded him. Reeling from the din of voices shouting in his head all at once, he closed his eyes and shut his mind to them. He would have to get whatever information he needed the conventional way.

Little groups of people flocked together in the crowded room, talking. He wandered from one group to the other, listening to the conversations. He heard chatter about trade, unfamiliar jokes, and idle chitchat from people who picked up the threads after a long time. But none of that helped find Amber. His wanderings took him to the bar, where he paid for a cider and sat on a stool to drink it. A man dressed in black leather approached the bar and stood next to Kal.

"A beer," he said to the barman.

"Hey, you're back!" said the barman. "Good hunt?"

"Very good. The Chief is also coming back tomorrow, and we have a nice surprise for him. A juicy one."

"Young?" the barman inquired.

"Young and fresh," the man said, laughing.

"Aha," the barman laughed as well.

"I need to go back and keep an eye on her, but boy, did I need this beer!" he said.

What the man had said could mean nothing or everything, and Kal thought frantically about what to do. He opened his mind, trying to get some impression from the man, but the clamor of the crowd's thoughts made it impossible. All he could see was the image of a young woman who could have been Amber or anyone else. He shut his mind to the surrounding thoughts. The man had dropped a coin on the counter and was walking out. Walking calmly to avoid looking conspicuous, Kal reached the exit. He positioned himself behind a carriage that was unloading merchandise. The trading post grounds sloped down toward a large esplanade. From his position behind the carriage, he had a good view of it, and he saw the man walking toward a structure at its far end. It was a wooden structure, like one of the barns that Kal had seen in an old documentary on ancient rural life. The man took up a position on a bench outside the building's door. Much as he tried, Kal couldn't distinguish any thoughts coming from inside the barn over the background noise. He tried to change position, but to no avail. He had to get closer.

——————— · —— · ———————

Kal was determined to find out what or who was inside that barn. He would stay there, no matter how long it took, but he feared making himself conspicuous. He had to find someplace to pass the time until dark. And then he'd have to find a way to get closer and find out if Amber was in that barn. A grumbling sound coming from his stomach reminded him how sparingly he had eaten lately. He was hungry from the long walk and decided to find a place to eat while passing the time. It was late, and the light was fading, so walking around felt somehow safer than before. He crossed the esplanade toward one of the streets that wound between single-story buildings. Most of the buildings were made of wood, with mud walls, and had few windows opening to the street.

A short walk took Kal to a small square. At one end, music and light came from two open windows of a three-story building. Kal approached one of the windows and peeped inside. The place was a mess, dotted with tables of all sizes and shapes. Instead of having sanitary serving machines, food was served by people. It reminded him of a school lesson about the ancient customs of barbarian populations. A whole wall was taken up by a counter and by shelves loaded with bottles. The room was crowded enough for Kal to feel reassured that he would not be noticed.

Inside, he selected a small table in a quiet corner and sat down to observe the scene. He had settled down for less than a minute before a young woman approached him. She wore a short skirt above long legs and a shirt that did a lousy job of covering her generous breasts. She was plump, and Kal couldn't help gazing at her figure. In The City, the H-cubicle ensured you stayed lean, keeping body mass at a healthy level. Still, he was surprised to realize that her rounded curves were pleasing to the eye. Her hair was a flaming red, and he couldn't help noticing her purple-lacquered fingernails. As she addressed him, Kal felt that he was blushing. The unisex uniforms worn in The City did not expose any body part that could embarrass the public. To him, the overt display of her body was almost shocking.

"Hello, dear," she greeted him, "what will it be?"

"I don't know. I'm new here."

"We have many options," she said, smiling.

Kal was starting to regret walking in like that. *Options?* In his previous life—which felt like years away—he never had to make decisions on food. The Department of Nutrition dictated the menu, and he always felt satisfied after a meal. But now he knew the satisfaction was artificial, merely the product of a stimulus delivered to his brain by his chip.

"Like what?" he asked. He had no idea what she was talking about and needed more information to get out of this.

"Drink or food?"

"Food."

"Well, I can give you today's specials here for two silver pieces. Or … if you prefer a bit more privacy, I can serve it to you in one of our upstairs rooms for five silver pieces. You're cute," she added, seeing that he was hesitating, "and I hope you'll take the private room."

Kal hesitated. Five silver pieces would make a big dent in his small coffer, but several people had already gazed at him. That worried him that he might be noticed. Getting away from the public eye could be worth the price. Another option was to walk out, but that would make him even more conspicuous. Besides, he was hungry.

"I'll eat in the private room," he said.

"Perfect. Go up the stairs. My room is number five. Here's the key. Make yourself comfortable," she said and turned away.

Kal was already feeling better. *This is a hospitable town*, he thought. People were friendly and thoughtful, and perhaps he didn't need to worry so much.

CHAPTER 14

Up in room number 5, Kal found a tiny table with a wooden chair, a large bed, and a washbasin filled with water. After the long walk in the heat of the day, washing his face in it felt good. He used the water sparingly, hoping that she wouldn't think he was taking a liberty with it. She was so nice, and he didn't want to come across as impolite, but he had at least to wash his hands before eating. That was the protocol in The City. He sat on the chair and waited. Time passed, and finally the door opened, and the woman came in with a tray. A soup bowl on the tray diffused a delicious smell, and so did a hot loaf of bread. Kal's stomach grumbled in response to them.

"I've put a good chunk of meat in the soup so that you can keep your strength up. But why didn't you make yourself comfortable on the bed? That chair is hard."

"Oh, I wouldn't take the liberty—"

She gave him a strange look, placed the tray on the table, then took a step back and gazed at him.

"What's your name?" she asked.

"Kal. I'm Kal, and you?"

"I'm Dora. Go ahead and eat that before it gets cold."

Kal nodded and picked up the spoon. He was hungry, and the food was delicious. He ate while she watched him. She sat on the bed, only a step away. Eating under somebody's probing eyes felt weird. In The City's public dining rooms, everybody kept their eyes on their food. Staring at people eating was considered unthinkably rude. Even just looking straight at people was not done. You had no business making people uncomfortable.

"That was very good, thanks," he said when all the food was gone.

"You need to pay me now," she said.

"I ... yes, of course. I'm sorry," he said, feeling that he was blushing again and trying to fight it. He reached into his purse and came out with five pieces of silver. She took them and placed them in a small bag that hung from her belt.

"Come here," she ordered, patting the bed. "Come," she said again when he hesitated.

Kal started to worry that her behavior was a little strange. He had got what he paid for and was full, so much so that he felt a bit groggy. He was happy to linger and kill some time. He wasn't planning to go back to the barn until much later. He wasn't sure about the proper etiquette for making conversation with a waitress after a meal. In The City, waitresses did not exist, except in Sector Five, which he never visited. And you didn't get to make conversation with the food-dispensing machine. Still, Dora had been kind to him, and he didn't want to offend her, so he got up and stood by the bed. She also stood up. She was almost his height and looked him over openly, making him blush for the third time. She unbuttoned her blouse, exposing her large breasts.

Kal gawked at her. He had never been close to a woman who was not fully covered. He, of course, knew everything about reproduction, how that worked, and the role of the breasts. He had learned it from educational videos. The Department of Guidance selected them and sent them to his home viewing system in preparation for his mating year. But he had never experienced anything akin to desire. He knew that when the time came, and he married the mate selected for him, the system would deliver the appropriate stimuli to his chip. The reproductive stimuli would trigger animal instincts in his brain, motivating him to procreate. They would continue only for the time needed to perpetuate the species. But now—now, in a flash, he understood what "animal instincts" meant, and it had nothing to do with reproduction.

"Let me help you," said Dora as she started to unbutton his shirt.

"No!" Kal cried. He stepped away from her, sat in the chair, and put his face in his hands.

"What's the matter? Did I do anything wrong?"

"No, no. It's not you; it's me," Kal whispered between his fingers, still hiding his face.

"I don't understand. Don't you want me?"

"No, I didn't mean ...."

"I don't get it. Why did you want to come up to my room, then?"

"I only wanted some quiet, to eat alone. That's all. I didn't understand that ... that it meant something else."

"Oh, boy. Where do you come from, the moon? Everybody around here knows what 'going up' means. Well," she added, "I'm not giving you any money back, you know?"

"I don't want it back. I'm sorry for making all this trouble."

"No trouble. Less work. But you're cute, and I'd do it for you for free."

She approached him and pulled his hands away from his face. She was smiling, and Kal felt a little better, seeing that she was not angry.

"You look troubled, and you're pale. What's the matter with you?"

"Nothing. I can't say. Can I stay in the room a little longer to rest?"

"Sure, you paid for it. As long as I don't need it for work. But if I do, you're out of here in a flash, agreed?"

Kal nodded and, for the first time, managed a smile. Before he knew what was happening, Dora leaned forward and planted a kiss on his lips.

"Say goodbye before you go," she said and left.

Kal sat there, staring at the door. He was starting to understand that the future held many unknowns in store for him. He would have to face problems that he had never had to confront when the chip regulated his life. Only now did he realize the many dilemmas that the chip had spared him. Like, for instance, what to do when, without warning, you feel attracted to a woman like he now was to Dora.

———— • —— • ————

Kal was almost ready to go now. He had watched the sunset over an hour before, and itched to go and find out if Amber was in that barn. The door opened, and Dora walked in, a serious expression on her face. She closed the door silently behind her, then leaned against it and faced him.

"What will I do with you?" she asked.

"What do you mean?"

"Who are you?"

"I'm nobody. I'm a man passing through this place."

"So why is everybody looking for you?"

"Looking for me? I don't know anybody here. Who could be looking for me?"

"Listen. One of the traders, who calls himself Abe, has been drinking to celebrate a successful trading day. He tells everybody who will listen that he even sold clothes to a city person. One of the Chief's guards heard him and called others. City people are not welcome around here. But I get the sense that you are something more than a simple City person. Perhaps you are a spy or something. They are looking everywhere for you. If they find you here, I will be in big trouble, so tell me why I shouldn't call them and give you away."

"No, please, don't do that!"

If you weren't so cute, I'd kick you out in a second. Without planning to, Kal had opened his mind to Dora's thoughts. He didn't know whether to feel alarmed or reassured by what he had heard.

"I won't, but if you keep going around clueless as you are, they'll catch you pretty soon anyway."

Kal sat heavily on the bed. He knew that she was right. He didn't stand a chance in that place that was so foreign to him. Any time he tried to behave like a local, he blundered.

"You're right; I know that."

"I can help you, though."

"How?"

"I can tell Al, who owns this place, that you are my cousin from Peace Hill. Al is looking for a busboy, and I can ask him to hire you. That will give you a harmless identity, and once you work here, nobody will pay attention to you. Besides, the town is full of people from all over today. After that Abe person leaves, nobody will be able to say where you came from or when you got here. What do you say?"

"Would you do that for me?"

"I offered to do it a moment ago."

"Why?"

"Let's say that I like you, and I don't care much for the Chief and his thugs. They've gotten under my skin more than once, and I'm surely not going to help them with anything."

"But I don't know anything about Peace Hill. Where is that?"

"It's far enough that nobody will make inquiries about you. If you're asked, tell everybody that it's up north in the mountains, and it takes two weeks to get here by horse carriage. If they insist on asking questions, tell them that the people of Peace Hill take a vow never to talk about their town. Tell them that talking about it is bad luck and may bring another Pulse upon you."

"Is that true?"

"Of course not! But Komsk's people are simpletons and will believe anything you tell them. People who live in Peace Hill are famously weirdos who venerate the earth and keep to themselves. All you have to do is keep silent, fix your gaze to the floor, and answer any question in monosyllables. You will be perfect for the part."

"I don't know how to thank you."

"You don't have to."

"I'll take your offer, and I'm forever in your debt. But first, I have to go out to check on something."

"That's not smart. If they catch you ...."

"I know, but I have to. If I go now, I should be back in an hour."

Dora sighed. "You *are* weird. I won't ask you why and where you want to go—I don't want to know. Come with me," she ordered.

Kal picked up his rucksack and followed her. Dora opened the door and checked both ends of the corridor before stepping out.

"We're going to the roof. From there, you can go down the fire escape, which will take you to the back of the building. I'll leave the roof door unlocked, and you can come back the same way when you're done. Quick, now!"

A flight of stairs at the end of the corridor took them to a door that opened to a roof. Walking carefully in the darkness, they reached the edge of the roof. The fire escape was nothing more than a metal ladder. Kal couldn't see all the way down, but he had to trust that the steps reached all the way. It made sense that they should. He grabbed the top of the ladder and prepared to descend.

"One moment!" Dora whispered.

She got close and, before Kal understood what was happening, she put a hand on the nape of his neck, pulled him to her, and kissed him. It was a long, wet, and sensuous kiss that took him entirely by surprise. He had never kissed or been kissed before, and for a moment, he was completely disoriented. At last, she let go of him and took a step back, smiling.

"I needed to get that out of my system," she said. "Now go before anybody comes along and sees you."

Kal nodded—it was all he could do—and then he started climbing down the ladder. The back of the building and the street were pitch dark, and he stopped about midway down. He had to make sure that nobody was waiting for him there, so he opened his mind to nearby thoughts. He picked up a few faint ones from inside the building, but nothing ominous from the outside. He made it to the bottom of the ladder, landing on the dirt street. At first, he was a bit disoriented. He had to think hard before he realized which direction would lead him to the barn. Then he walked toward the least-lighted area.

CHAPTER 15

The Chief Executive was back. He enjoyed his title, which he thought became him. He used to joke with his wife that it was much better than "Chief Brigand," which was closer to what he was. He was a smart man, though. He had come to Komsk with a handful of "operatives," as he liked to call them. He had gotten himself elected mayor within a few weeks, following the mysterious disappearance of the incumbent. Everybody who got in his way disappeared as if by magic, never to be heard from again, and the population got the hint. Under his rule, Komsk had grown from a small fracking station to a prosperous town and a center of commerce for the surrounding territories. Residents loved him for that and kept a blind eye to his less appealing side. He knew not to scare away activities that helped the town prosper and fill his coffers. He kept a short beard and long, unkempt hair that gave him a wild look. The addition of his yellow teeth made him a scary person to look at.

Soon after his arrival, he had taken a wife. He was partial to her (he never spoke in terms of "love," a sentiment foreign to him). True, she was capricious, noisy, and sometimes a pain in the neck, but he wouldn't give her up. He knew that he was to blame for spoiling her and letting her get everything she wanted. She reciprocated by not complaining about his vices. She didn't bitch when he enjoyed the company of her maids, but she had a habit of getting rid of the ones he liked best and visited most often. They had an unspoken arrangement that worked well for both, and his policy had always been to leave well enough alone.

Amber was almost glad when the door opened to let a man in. She had been cooped up in that barn for too long without knowing what was in store for her. The uncertainty of her situation was eating at her. She had inspected every inch of the barn, looking for an escape route. It soon became clear to her that there was none. Marion had given up trying to encourage her while she paced the barn like a caged animal. Now she was sitting on the floor, holding her knees between her hands.

"Get up!" the man ordered. "Not you," he added, addressing Marion.

Amber got to her feet and gazed at him. He was one of the guards who had brought them food before. "What do you want?" she asked.

"You're coming with me," was the curt answer.

Amber knew resisting was futile and allowed the man to lead her by the arm. Outside, he closed and bolted the door. Then he pushed her unkindly toward the street, leading to a constructed area. They reached a three-story building and stopped at a door guarded by two men.

"The Chief is waiting for us," said the man from the barn.

One of the guards nodded and opened the door to let them in. Inside, the man from the barn pointed to a bench.

"Sit down. You will be summoned," he ordered.

Amber sat. She was too tired to argue and too worried about what lay ahead. She had slept only for a short time, jumping up at every noise. Now she felt emptied of her usual strength and at the mercy of her captors. Her guard stood a little away from her, leaning against the wall and, from time to time, directing an empty glance toward her. After what seemed to Amber to be a long time, a door opened, and a man came out. He gestured to her guard to come, and he stirred from his dreamy state.

"Move," he said. He grabbed her by the arm and propelled her toward the door. Amber walked mechanically, breathing small, shallow breaths, feeling the apprehension mount in her.

Inside, the large room was poorly lit. A man sat behind a wooden table that could seat twelve, which was loaded with remains of a meal. He was drinking from a large cup, and when she walked in, he put it down and gazed at her.

"What do we have here?" he asked with a smirk.

"This is the girl that we found at C-54, Chief," said the guard.

"And what were you doing there?"

"Nothing," said Amber. She had given a lot of thought to the story that she had to tell. One thing was clear: she couldn't let anybody know who she was and where she was coming from.

"Don't play games with me," said the Chief. "You don't live at C-54. Why were you there?"

"I am Sarah's niece. Sarah, who runs C-54," she added when a look of puzzlement made it clear that the name meant nothing to him. "I came to stay with her after my mother died. We lived on a small farm up north. It was in ruins already before my mother died, and there was nothing to keep me there."

She had hoped that he wouldn't be interested enough to demand more details of where she had lived before, and he wasn't.

"Mmm ... I don't know what I'll do with you."

"Perhaps I can use her." The voice came from the dark end of the room. Amber hadn't noticed the woman sitting there until she got up. "Let me see her," she added. She approached and inspected Amber closely. She placed her hand under her chin and made her lift her head.

"Yes, she could be my new maid. The temporary help I've had since the other one went is a disaster. I'll take her."

"Are you sure?" asked the Chief. "You weren't happy with the last one you picked, either."

"We'll see. You're lucky," she said, speaking to Amber, "very lucky. Make sure not to disappoint me."

"Oh, all right. Take her if you like," said the Chief. "Now go, I'm busy."

"Take her to the servants' quarters," said the woman to the guard, and then she went back to sit in the dark.

Kal's timing was unfortunate. Had he come only a few minutes earlier, he would have seen Amber leave with the guard. Instead, he had watched the barn for a few minutes without seeing anybody. The guard who was there before had disappeared, and the place was silent. He ran to the door and checked the lock. It was bolted from the outside, and he could open it easily. But first, he needed to make sure that Amber was inside. He opened his mind, searching for distinct thoughts. He heard thoughts coming from inside the barn, which he realized meant that only one person was there. The images he received were confused, and he couldn't be sure that they came from Amber. Beside the door, he saw a barred window and peered inside. The indistinct shape of a woman lying on the floor was all he could see in the darkness. It had to be Amber, though. Moving without hesitation, he unbolted the door and walked in. The figure got up with a jerk at the sound of his entrance.

"Amber!" he called.

"Who are you?" came the answer, and Kal's heart fell when he heard that it wasn't Amber's voice.

"I came for Amber. Do you know her?"

"Yes, she was here with me, but a short while ago, a guard came for her. I don't know where they took her."

"Why are you here?"

"They captured me. It's a long story. Can you help me? I need to get away before they come for me."

"Go. The door is open. There's nobody to keep you."

"It's useless. What good will it do to run away on foot? If they come soon and discover that I've fled, they'll catch up with me in no time. I need some way to put at least a few miles between me and this place. Running away and getting caught again will make things worse for me."

Kal considered. He had an idea that might help her, but he had his own problems to face. Still, he needed to stick around and see if Amber was coming back.

"I can't help you with transportation, but I can make them believe that you're still in there and buy you time. If they don't come inside, you'll be okay."

"Are you sure? How can you do that?" Marion sounded worried.

"No time to explain. Go!"

"I don't know how to thank you. If I make it, I'd like to do something for you. Seek me out in Electric City. My name is Marion. The man I'm going to marry owns the Universal Electronic Repair Shop. He's an important person there."

"All right, I will, but quit talking and run—now."

Marion nodded and left. Kal closed and bolted the door and took a position in the dark next to the nearest building. He felt tired and had to fight to keep his eyes open. After a while, the sound of steps brought him back to alertness. Kal's heart sank—the guard was back, but without Amber. He took his position at the door again. There was really no point in Kal remaining there now that Amber was gone, but he had promised Marion he would help her. After a few minutes, the guard got up from his chair and went to look inside through the little window. Kal concentrated. He hoped that the image of a sleeping woman that he was projecting would be credible. The man looked through the window for what Kal thought was too long, but he seemed satisfied. He went back to his chair and lay back, closing his eyes. Kal couldn't help but smile, thinking of the surprise that awaited him in the morning.

———

Amber's guard had sent for someone he called the "house manager," a middle-aged woman with a beaked nose. They had taken Amber to the third floor, to a door guarded by another armed guard, who turned a heavy key in the lock and let them in.

"The girls will give you clothes. Go and get a bath—you stink."

With those words, the woman left, closing the door behind her. She had barely glanced at Amber all the way up. Amber heard the key turn in the lock. She stood at the door, taking in the room and its contents. The atmosphere was one of calm, with comfortable seats, low lighting, and two young women sitting on a couch. The air was scented in pleasant contrast to the stinking barn. One of the two young women got up from her couch and approached her.

"Hey!" she said with a welcoming smile.

She sounded friendly, and Amber smiled reflexively. "Hi," she answered.

"What's your name?"

"I'm Amber. You?"

"I'm Faith, and that is Gloria. How did you get here?"

"I was at the C-54 station when these men raided it. They captured me and took me here. Now I'm told that I should be some woman's maid. That's all I know."

"The Lady's maid? Oh, my! Now I understand why they took that poor girl away."

"Which poor girl?"

"The one who was the Lady's maid before you got here. I'm afraid—"

"What?"

"Nothing. Doesn't matter. What is C-54?"

"It is—was a travel lodge. They raided it and killed everybody but me."

"Poor thing! Well, let's get you organized, as the house manager said."

"That odious woman?"

"She's not too bad ... if you know how to handle her. Anyway, come here. There is a bath in that room over there, and frankly, you really need to take one."

"I know. I'm dying for a bath."

"There is a large closet in that room. There you'll find clothes. Pick anything you like. They're all for our use. Meanwhile, I'll fix you something to eat. I'm sure you're hungry."

"I'm starving; how did you know?"

"I've been in the barn myself," said Faith.

Amber took a step toward the bathroom and then stopped. "Faith—"

"Yes?"

"What is this place? What do you do here?"

Faith hesitated for a moment. "Go take your bath," she said at last. "I'll tell you everything later."

CHAPTER 16

Kal was desperate. He didn't know what to do now that Amber was gone, God knew where. All he could do was hope that nothing bad would happen to her until he found out where she was. But for now, going on to roam the streets, endangering himself, was pointless. He went back to the restaurant, climbed up the fire escape, and found the door unlocked, as promised. He tiptoed to Dora's door, opened it silently, and closed it behind him with a sigh of relief.

"You're back," said Dora.

"As I told you I would. Why are you surprised?"

"I'm used to men who don't keep their promises and never come back."

"I do."

"You're a gem," she said, smiling. "Now we need to think about what to do with you tonight. Tomorrow I can ask Al to hire you and to give you someplace to sleep, but tonight we'll have to manage."

"I can sleep on the floor," Kal volunteered.

"No need for that. The bed is large enough for both of us if you don't toss and turn too much when you sleep."

"You don't mind?"

Dora gave him a scornful look and didn't respond. Instead, she started to undress.

"I've had a long day, made longer by waiting up for you, and tomorrow is another long day. Let's get some sleep."

Kal averted his gaze, embarrassed, and waited.

"Are you going to stand there all night? Get undressed and come under the blanket. Nights get cold around here."

Kal nodded, removed his shoes, shirt, and trousers, and got into bed with his back to Dora.

"You do know how grateful I am to you for all you're doing," he murmured.

"Well, then, the least you can do is to look at me when you speak. I don't like to talk to your back."

Kal turned to face her. "I'm sorry," he said.

"Stop being sorry about everything. It's annoying."

"I'm s—. I won't."

She gazed intensely into his eyes, making him blush.

"Who are you, Kal?"

"I'm ... nobody."

Dora gave him a sideways glance.

"Come here, let me see something," she ordered. When Kal got closer, she ran a hand through his hair, right above his right ear. She massaged it with the tip of her fingers, then pulled her hand away. "I can't feel it—I mean, the scar from the implantation of the chip. But you know what I think? I think you are an important person, a fugitive from The City who's hiding here, I don't know why. Am I right?"

Kal hesitated. His instinct told him that the less they spoke about him and the less she knew, the better. But he was at her mercy, and she was onto him. Besides, she had been helping him, and without her help, he would be in big trouble. He had to tell her the truth, or at least the part she needed to know.

"They did a good job when they implanted my chip, and I was

only one year old, an age when your body heals well. The scar is there, but it's difficult to find if you don't know how." He stopped for a moment and gazed at Dora, who showed no surprise and waited in silence for him to go on speaking. "You are right, at least in part. I have escaped from The City."

"I knew it! What are you running from? All I know about The City is that you people live a great life with all the comforts of technology, not like us, who hang on to old technology that is rotting away and have no prospects for the future. Nobody in the Surroundings knows anything about science or technology. The best they can do is to fix the old equipment, and that only works sometimes. It's not like where you come from, with all your fancy technology. Everybody here would want to become a City citizen; only, no one can get into The City and settle down there. It's no secret that they can spot a foreigner in a second, and when they do, you're as good as dead. People have tried it because of all the great things you can have there. Nobody has ever come back to brag about making it, though. So you must have a good reason for giving all that up."

"It's not so nice and pleasant as you think. At least, it isn't when you find out the reality of what is going on. It's tyranny. It's true that you're well looked after as long as you are useful to the tyrants. But if you stop being useful or fall out of line, there will be no mercy for you. I've fallen out of line, so I had to run away, but I'm not important. I'm nobody, I swear."

Dora sat up and gazed at him for a long time before speaking again.

"No. I know that's not true," she said at last. "You're not a nobody; you're special. There is something special about you, and I want to find out what it is."

"Believe me, I'm a regular man who is in trouble. And if it weren't for you, I'd probably be done for. I can't tell you how grateful I am."

Dora smiled a teasing smile. "Don't tell me. Show it to me."

"Ah?"

"Hold me. Hold me like you care about me."

"I ... I don't know how. I've never been so close to a woman."

Dora gave a little laugh, and then, leaning on her elbow, she gently stroked his cheek with her hand.

"A virgin. I haven't met one in years! Let me show you how it's done," she said.

CHAPTER 17

Alvin paced the room restlessly. It had been two days already since he had given orders to find Sazar's daughter, and nobody knew where she was. He stopped when the door opened to admit Larkin. His smug smile usually meant that he had news.

"Well?" Alvin snapped at him. Waiting was taking its toll on his nerves. Larkin knew him well enough and spoke soothingly.

"We have sent word everywhere. We have contacts in the Surroundings, as far as Portfort—imagine that! Communications are difficult, as you know. The Pulse destroyed most of the communication equipment in the Surroundings, and what remains is in poor repair. Still, we managed to distribute Sazar's daughter's picture to quite a few locations."

"And? What have you heard? Don't keep me waiting, damn you!"

"Sorry," said Larkin with a smile that belied the truthfulness of the sentiment. "I only now heard back from two places where we have agents. They say that the girl may be there."

"She can't be in two places at the same time."

"Obviously. At least one of our agents is wrong, but the other may be right. I'm waiting for more information. I've sent both of them a picture of the girl's tattoo. Perhaps that will help."

"All right. But we may be wasting precious time. What if she's there but gets away before we find her? That's too dangerous. You need to send someone to pick her up now."

"That's dangerous, too. You know that we are not loved by the barbarians out there, to put it mildly. Approaching the rulers of any place outside The City requires careful planning. We need to think this through."

"Well, do that! Don't waste any more time."

Alvin turned around to hide his anger. Larkin was becoming too independent for his own good. And too cocky. He would have to do something about it.

"I'm sorry if I have failed to act swiftly enough. As you wish," Larkin said servilely. "I'll make some plans and will be back soon to have you approve them."

"Good. I appreciate it," said Alvin, mollified by Larkin's show of respect. He didn't mind that Larkin was faking it.

"Lieutenant Oliver."

Larkin addressed the young Immaculate officer who stood at attention before him. "I am about to entrust you with a critical and delicate mission."

"Anything, sir, of course," said the young man.

"I appreciate your earnest approach to this, but you shouldn't underestimate the complexity and the danger. I need you to take a surveillance capsule and go to a settlement in the Surroundings. The exact location is not important right now, and I will share it with you as soon as it is finalized. There, you will have to locate and bring back a subject. The subject in question is a young woman. This is her picture, and I'm beaming it to your information gear so you'll have it handy for identifying her. I am also sending you this other image," he added, showing a picture of Amber's tattoo. "This is a tattoo—I know, it's abhorrent," he said, seeing the young man flinch, "but it will help you to identify her positively. She has it on her right shoulder. Is that clear?"

"Yes, sir. She's a barbarian, then. A chipless, I gather."

"Correct. Do you have any other questions?"

The young officer hesitated for a moment. Questioning orders was not something done lightly. He appeared to be having trouble finding words.

"If I may, sir," he said, at last, speaking with hesitation, "I wonder, why not take a larger air vehicle? The surveillance capsule is slow and can only fly four. That means that I will only be able to take two more officers with me, given that we need room for this young woman. Also, if we run into problems, we will only have light weapons. The capsule can't carry heavy ones, and we may find ourselves at a disadvantage."

"That's a good question and to the point. Let me explain. This is not going to be a raid. We hope there will be no active hostility. This is a diplomatic mission. You will have negotiating power, and we expect you to win the cooperation of the relevant ruling individuals. Of course, you must be ready in case you encounter resistance. If you have to use your weapons to disengage, you'll know what to do, but we hope it won't be necessary. We trust your common sense and ability."

"I understand, sir. I will not disappoint you."

"I'm sure you won't," said Larkin, but it sounded more like a threat than a vote of confidence.

———

Amber had finally fallen asleep after tossing and turning for a long time. It was not the bed, which was comfortable, that kept her awake, or the atmosphere, which was actually quite nice, with subdued lighting and pleasant scents. It was what Faith had told her. Amber had lingered in the bath, enjoying every moment, and Faith had brought her food and a beverage. Then, she sat down with Amber while she ate and explained how things were done in that house.

The mistress, the Chief's wife, was mean and capricious. Faith cautioned that Amber should never, under any circumstances, talk back to her. Proud girls didn't survive for long in that place. On the positive side, it was light work. She didn't have many needs, and the girls took turns helping her get dressed, with her makeup, and other basic needs. Sometimes she took one of the girls out with her. That was the only opportunity they had to alleviate the boredom. Otherwise, they remained confined to their apartments most of the time.

The Chief was another story. From time to time, he would summon one of the girls to his quarters "for entertainment." When that happened, the best thing that Amber could do was detach her mind from her body. Faith recommended thinking pleasant thoughts and waiting it out. She had been there three times and knew what she was talking about. It was unpleasant, she said, but she survived, and so would Amber. Amber didn't think so, and the thought kept her awake until fatigue forced her into a disturbed sleep.

———————

The night guard thought he was lucky to get the guard duty that night. He had switched with a friend who had been more than happy to oblige. His job as an all-purpose guard to the Chief allowed him to gather information without arousing suspicion. Being a City spy was not heavy work, but it was dangerous. The Chief would skin him alive if he found out, but so far, he had never had a reason to suspect him. All he did was send periodic reports to The City—when the communication equipment was working, that is. The only thing that might give him away was his small transmitter. So he kept other broken electronic equipment in his room. He had staged a hobbyist workshop to have a good story ready to explain the transmitter away if it was ever found. His task for that night was different. It would put him where he wasn't supposed to be, which meant possible trouble. He turned the key in the heavy lock as silently as possible and pushed the door open. He was not allowed to go into the women's quarters, but he had his story ready. If someone inquired, he would say that he had heard strange noises and had gone in to investigate.

"Psss ..." he hissed into the room.

"Who's there?" came a woman's voice from the darkness.

"What was that noise?" the guard asked.

"What noise?"

"It's Faith, right? That's your name?"

"So?"

"Come over here; I don't want to shout and wake everybody up."

Faith approached the door and gazed at the guard unwelcomingly.

"What noise?" she repeated.

"I don't know. A strange one. Who's in here?"

"Only me and the other girls."

"Who, the new one?"

"Her too."

"I'm told she's a strange one, a witch. They say that she has a satanic tattoo on her shoulder."

"What are you, an old woman?" Faith said, speaking with open scorn.

"No, I'm serious. Have you seen it? They say it's the inverted pentagram in a circle, the sign of the devil!"

"She doesn't have anything like that, stupid! Her tattoo is cute

—it's a sun with a smiling face in a circle. You have cockeyed friends."

"Oh, okay. Nothing to worry about, then. Go back to sleep," he said and closed and locked the door. He congratulated himself on being so cunning. He waited impatiently for his shift to end so that he could send the good news to his masters.

CHAPTER 18

K al got up, feeling far from rested. He had slept fitfully at the edge of the bed, trying not to get too close to Dora. He had allowed her to hug him and cuddle him until she fell asleep, but her fondling of him had left him embarrassed and uncomfortable. He dressed in silence, then sat in the chair, waiting for her to wake up. Despite all his attempts to avoid making noise, Dora stirred and sat up.

"Uhmm, up already?" she asked, opening one eye.

"Yes, for a while. Good morning."

"Yeah. We'll see," she said. "Wait here," she added and walked out.

When she returned, she washed her face in the small basin, then gestured for him to help himself to it. Kal looked at the water in the basin. He had always lived in a sanitized environment, and using water polluted by somebody else went against his very nature. Still, Dora was gazing at him, and he didn't want to offend her. He dipped his fingers into the basin of water and then perfunctorily passed them over his closed eyes.

"Later I'd like to find someplace to wash properly," he said in a low voice.

"As soon as Al has hired you, you'll be able to go and take a shower," she said. "Now, let's go get something to eat."

Dora took him to the kitchen, which, at that hour of the day, was empty. She motioned for him to sit at a small table in a corner, picked up a pan, and started to fry eggs with bacon. Kal had seen people do it in old movies, but he never expected to see it done in real life. He also never dreamed that he would eat the results of such unhealthy cooking. His home cooker always supplied him with clean, healthy food with the right amount of proteins and other nutrients. It was the modern, if not tasty, way of eating. That's how everybody ate in The City, but he had to admit that the smell from the stove was much more inviting. He had never seen an egg close up. He picked one up, smelled it, and put it back.

"Eggs don't smell," Dora said, laughing.

"I've never seen one before," said Kal. "It's amazing."

"Oh, boy! You haven't lived yet."

Dora split the food between two plates, put a loaf of brown bread on the table, and poured coffee into two cups. She sat down and started to tuck into her breakfast. Kal gazed at her, a fork in his hand. She stopped eating.

"What's the matter? Aren't you hungry?"

"Yes, I'm famished. But this is not the kind of food I'm used to."

"You'd better get used to it fast because this is what you'll get for breakfast."

Kal nodded and put a forkful of scrambled egg into his mouth.

"It's delicious!" he exclaimed.

"Yes, they tell me that I'm good with the skillet," said Dora with open satisfaction.

The door opened, and a middle-aged man came in.

"Morning, Al," said Dora, speaking casually.

"Who's this?" the man blurted out. "Are you bringing in vagabonds for me to feed again?"

"No, Al. And don't be an ass. This is my cousin, Kal, who

came to visit me to bring me news of the family in Peace Hill. I know that you're looking for help in the restaurant, and I was waiting for you to get up so I could talk to you about it. Kal plans to stay in town for a while before going back home and needs a job. You need a busboy, so what do you say?"

"Uhmm ..." said Al, turning to Kal. "I could use some help around here right now. The pay isn't much—just food, shelter, and a little pocket money. If that's what you're looking for, you can start when you're through feeding your face."

"Yes, sir. Thank you, sir. I appreciate it."

"All right. That's enough. No need to go all thankful on me. It's annoying. Now make yourself useful," he added, turning to Dora, "and cook some of that garbage for me."

———— • ——— • ————

Kal was fit, but he had never done any real physical work. By bedtime that night, his body ached in several places. His back was stiff from lifting boxes of incoming supplies and all the leaning forward he had to do while washing kitchenware. Still, he felt good and strangely satisfied. He had spent a whole day doing menial work ill-befitting a scientist like him, and he found it fulfilling. *Strange*, he thought. Al had assigned him a tiny room on the same floor as Dora's. He had taken a long shower in what didn't look at all like a shower to him. At home, all he had to do was undress and go into his H-cubicle. While taking his body's health measurements, the built-in system pleasantly massaged him with a balanced mixture of water and detergent, dispensed at the perfect temperature. That was followed by a stream of pure water that caressed his body before warm air dried him up. Here, in contrast, the water temperature alternated between scorching hot and freezing cold. The window did not close well and let in a stream of cold air that made him shiver. To make it even more uncomfortable, all he had available to dry himself was a coarse towel. Still, it was great. He felt alive like he had never felt before.

Now back in his room, Kal sat on the bed to think. He hadn't had an opportunity to speak with Dora during the day, although they had worked in the same space. The trading week had come to an end, and many traders had already left. Some had stayed longer to visit with family, to have some fun not available where they lived, or to drink themselves into stupefaction. As a result, the restaurant was busy during the day, and so were they. Dora was an enigma to Kal. She had done for him more than he would have expected from any stranger, and she asked nothing in return. That was not how things worked back in The City. Life had to be a balancing act. If someone did something for you, he or she expected something in return, and you looked forward to recipro-cating as soon as possible. Remaining in debt to someone who helped you, even with a trivial matter, was not done. You wanted to reciprocate without delay. And here, it was not about a simple favor—it was a matter of life or death. She had saved him from the Chief's minions, who would have arrested him with who knows what dire consequences. He wondered how he could ever repay her.

A knock on the door interrupted his musing and made him jump up. "Who's there?" he asked.

"It's me. Dora. May I come in?" came the voice from outside.

"Sure." Kal opened the door that he had locked—he felt safer that way—and Dora walked in.

"You've showered. Good," she said.

She, too, has been to the shower, Kal thought, noting her wet hair. She must have taken a really hot shower, he concluded, judging from the wave of warmth coming from her body. It was one of Kal's habits to note things, which helped him immensely in his work. Dora leaned with her back against the door and locked it, turning the key without looking.

"So, how was your first day?" she asked.

"I loved it! It was all so new and special," Kal said earnestly. "I'm so grateful to you. I don't know how to repay you ...."

"I know how," she said, getting a little closer.

"How?" Kal inquired. If there was something she needed done, he was eager to do it to repay his debt to her.

"Can you guess what I'm thinking?" she asked with a smile.

I know that it's wrong, and I shouldn't, Kal thought, *but all this is so unfamiliar to me that unless I read her mind, I won't know how to do the right thing by her.*

He opened his mind to her thoughts, and the meaning of her question hit him. His face reddened, and he gaped at her.

"I see that you guessed," she said, still smiling. Without waiting for a response, she pressed her body against his and kissed him. Kal didn't resist. He didn't know how to resist, and, what's more, he didn't want to.

"I—" Kal started to say, but she placed a finger on his lips.

"Shhh," she said. "I know that this is new to you. I'll be gentle."

Kal closed his eyes and didn't try to speak again. He didn't have anything worth saying anyway.

CHAPTER 19

Another day had passed, and now Kal waited impatiently for Dora to knock on his door again. She had opened up a whole new world to him. It was a world in which you reacted to people, not to a wave transmitted to the chip in your head. All the feelings and emotions that he had experienced the night before were new to him. He wanted more of them. He still tried to convince himself that it was his scientific curiosity talking. After all, shouldn't he be interested in examining the effect that external stimuli had on his brain? But he knew that he was kidding himself.

He tried to analyze his feelings for Dora. Did he love her? All he knew about love came from textbooks and old videos, but he thought he only "liked" her. The distinction was difficult for him, but he spent a lot of time formulating it for himself. He enjoyed being with her; he found her friendly, pleasant, and affectionate, but he didn't actually yearn to see her. He missed the physical contact for sure, but he didn't discover himself thinking fondly of her outside those times. So, he concluded, he didn't love her. He definitely liked her, though, and was forever grateful to her for opening up this new, wonderful world to him.

He also wondered whether she loved him. He didn't think so. From old videos, he had learned that females told their male companions when they loved them, and she hadn't said so. That was a relief. He wouldn't have known how to handle it.

He felt guilty that he hadn't given Amber a thought all day. He wondered what he should do. He had to find out what was happening to her, where she was being held, and what his options were for helping her escape. But thoughts of Dora had taken precedence over all that, and he felt terrible about it.

The door opened, and Dora came in, bringing a smile of welcome to Kal's lips. But the smile disappeared as soon as he saw the expression on her face.

"What's the matter? What happened?" he asked in a panic.

"You tell me. Since your arrival, the world has turned upside down. The town is in turmoil. Everybody is talking about a flying vehicle that has landed here in Komsk. Two men in white uniforms have come out of it."

"Immaculates!" Kal cried.

"You know who they are?"

"Tell me, did they wear white helmets that cover their faces?"

"I didn't see them, but from what I heard, that's correct."

"Then those are Immaculates. They must be after me. Only two, you said?"

"The man who saw them said that there was a third one who remained in the vehicle. If they are after you, how do they know that you are here?"

"I don't think they can know it. Maybe they are combing the provinces for me."

"And you said that you are not important!"

"I'm not important, but perhaps they think I am. Or they could be after somebody else."

As he said these words, Kal realized what they meant. They could be after Amber. He started to panic. If the Immaculates got hold of Amber, that would be the end of their hopes. He would never get to Freeland and develop the technology needed to fight the High Professor.

"Do you know where they went?" he asked.

"They must have gone to see the Chief. Nothing can be done in this town unless he agrees. So I guess they have to ask for his help, or at least for permission to search for you."

Kal got up and grabbed his rucksack.

"I have to go," he said in a low voice.

"Are you crazy? They'll kill you or capture you. You need to stay here and lie low, not to be out in the open."

"I must go. If they find me here, it will be trouble for you, and I can't allow it. And there is something else that I need to do."

"What?"

"You're better off not knowing, but trust me, I must."

"I'm scared." Dora was now shaking and held Kal's arm as if to stop him from going.

"I'll be okay, I promise."

"No, you won't. Stay with me!" Dora begged, still clinging to his arm.

"Please, Dora, please," said Kal, and she stepped back, letting go of him.

"You are going, after all ... Be careful. Promise me that you'll be careful."

"I promise. And I promise that I'll come back ... when I can."

"Yes, sure—"

Dora choked, turned around for a second, then turned back and kissed him.

"Go now," she said at last, and Kal nodded and left.

It was an hour after the last diner had left the restaurant, and the streets were empty. Whether that was because of the late hour or the unusual presence of the Immaculates, Kal couldn't say. He kept himself in the shade of the buildings until he reached the large square of the barn. A white capsule had landed in the middle of the yard, and an Immaculate sat behind the controls, gazing ahead.

He was too far for Kal to see the details, but close enough for him to see that the vizier on his helmet pointed in his direction. Any movement on his part would be detected by the helmet's image-processing software, which would alert the Immaculate to his presence. Kal lingered in the darkness, debating what to do. Before he tried anything, he realized that he had to find out what the other two Immaculates were doing. He backtracked into the maze of narrow streets and ran toward the Chief's mansion. Two armed men stood guard outside, and Kal remained in the dark so they wouldn't see him.

It was time to use his gift—he had come to call it that since he had learned to control it. He now opened his mind and listened. He had spent much of his working day exercising to isolate his thoughts from those of different people in the crowded restaurant. What he had learned during the day was now coming to his aid. He discounted the thoughts of the guards at the door and "moved" inside. If called upon to explain how his mind was touring different parts of the house, he wouldn't have been able to describe it. All he did was focus on moving forward or upward, and other thoughts reached him. It was all instinctive, and he didn't worry too much about it, as long as it served his needs. At last, he registered clearly relevant thoughts.

He's taking his sweet time with it, came a strong, clear thought. *He said that he would bring the girl himself already half an hour ago. We must be alert. I don't know what he's plotting.*

The thoughts carried a clear sense of fear and distress, and Kal knew they came from one of the Immaculates. He concentrated on this person and listened.

Here she is, the triumphant thought came after a short while. *She must be the one. She looks just like the girl in the picture. Show us her shoulder, you stupid!* After a short time, the image of Amber's tattoo reached him, and he knew for sure that it was her they were looking at.

Professor Larkin will be delighted, and I'll be the one to bring him the girl, came the jubilant thought. A shiver ran down Kal's spine at the thought of Amber in the hands of the infamous Larkin. He had to stop them!

He had heard enough. He ran back to the esplanade and to the capsule. When he reached the corner of the closest house, he stopped and concentrated. He formed an image of the High Professor in his head. That very same image was everywhere in The City, and he had seen it since he was a child, so recreating it in his mind was easy. Then he projected his thought toward the capsule with all his strength. The Immaculate, sitting in the pilot seat, gaped at the image of the High Professor. As soon as Kal was sure that the pilot had seen the vision, he concentrated on making it move. The High Professor made an imperious gesture, summoning the pilot to him. He then took a few steps toward the back of the capsule. The astonished pilot climbed out of the capsule and walked toward what he believed to be the High Professor.

"Sir, at your command, sir!" he barked.

Kal ran to the Immaculate and grabbed him by the throat from behind, making him drop his helmet. He planned to overpower him, tie him up, and hide him inside the capsule. But the pilot was fighting back with all his strength. A short struggle ended when, without intending to harm him, Kal twisted the pilot's neck so hard that it snapped. Time was short, and Kal had no time to process the shock of what he had done. He would have time to think about it later, when he and Amber were safe. He dragged the pilot's body, which luckily wasn't heavy, toward the empty barn. Inside, Kal undressed the pilot, piled straw over his body to hide him, and then dressed in his uniform. He was more or less his height, and the uniform fit him well. He then ran back to the capsule and got inside. A power gun hung from a stand by the pilot's seat. Kal checked it to make sure that it was ready for use. He turned the power switch to the "stun" position, and then he sat, waiting. Five minutes later, the two Immaculates arrived with

Amber between them, her hands tied. They walked up the capsule's hatch, pushing her before them.

"Stop pushing, you pig!" she cried, but one of the men pushed her harder.

"Sit down over here and keep quiet!" he ordered. "Hans, get ready to take off," he said, turning to the pilot's seat.

Amber's body was no longer between Kal and the two other men. He unlatched the gun and turned around.

"Stop playing with that gun, you idiot!" one of the men yelled. "What's the matter with you?"

"Now, you two step down and out of the capsule, slowly," said Kal.

The expression on the men's faces was one of astonishment.

"Are you out of your mind, Hans?" said one.

"He's not Hans," said the other.

"Who are you?" asked the first.

Slowly, before he notices, while he's busy speaking, came a clear thought. Alerted by it, Kal realized that the other Immaculate had drawn his gun and was about to point it at him. Instinctively, his finger pulled the trigger, and a blue ray hit the first man; as Kal turned the gun, it hit the second. Both Immaculates fell to the ground. The first one gave a few convulsions before stiffening, but the other fell to the floor without a cry. Kal was astonished and also a little elated by the success of his action. He hadn't realized the full power of the gun.

"Amber—," he said.

"Kal? How?" she managed to say.

Kal removed his helmet and went to untie her.

"Later," he said. "Later, I'll explain. Now we need to get away fast. Help me drag these two out of here, and then we must go."

"Did you kill them?"

"No, they're only stunned. They will be out for a few hours, I think. I've never used a stun gun myself, but I've read reports about it. We need to hide them, so our escape is not discovered before they come to."

"But ... do you know how to fly this thing?"

"A little ... at least, I hope. I've learned to fly a simpler version of this capsule during my basic training at the science academy. This is an Immaculate vehicle and is a bit different, but the basic functions should be the same. I recognize the controls. Now, let's get moving before somebody comes along."

Amber nodded and grabbed one of the Immaculates' feet. Kal lifted him by the shoulders, and together they dragged him out and into the nearby barn. Then they did the same with the second man.

"Here, let's tie them up with this rope," said Kal, showing a length of rope that he had picked up from the floor.

"Funny. This is the rope they used to tie me up with when they brought me here. Hey! What is this?"

The pilot's leg protruded from under the straw.

"Don't look," said Kal. "That was the pilot. I had to kill him. Not on purpose. It was an accident that happened when we struggled."

Amber looked at him with admiration and said nothing. Then she went on helping Kal tie the two Immaculates up.

Back in the capsule, Kal took the pilot's seat and fumbled with the commands. He found the one that closed the hatch, and then he turned on the engine.

"You'd better sit and buckle up," he said, fastening his own seat harness. "This may be a bumpy flight."

Amber came to stand before him. "Did I say 'thank you?'" she asked.

"No time for that now," Kal answered hastily.

"Thank you," said Amber, planting a kiss on his cheek. Then she sat in the copilot's seat, adjusted the harness straps, and buckled up.

Under Kal's inexpert hands, the capsule lifted off the ground and then suddenly flew into the darkness with a jolt.

CHAPTER 20

"What just happened?"

Amber's anguished question came as the capsule made a sharp turn just after a loud thud sounded from above. It seemed to slow in its flight.

"I don't know, but something's wrong with the commands. We are slowing down and losing height. Brace yourself. The altitude meter has gone wild, and I don't know when we will be hitting the ground."

Kal peered into the darkness. Trying to estimate how far they were from the ground was next to impossible. The moon was in its first quarter, and heavy clouds masked it and the stars. The ground below looked like a uniform, black surface. Kal didn't know where they were and hoped they weren't flying over the sea or another body of water. While escaping from Komsk, all that mattered to him was getting as far away as possible as quickly as possible. He had no idea how to operate the capsule's navigation equipment, and that wasn't the right time to learn.

"What can you do?"

"I'm slowing down as much as I can without dropping down. We will be going slowly when we hit the ground, and I hope the damage will be minimal. Now let me concentrate," he added, speaking with a confidence he didn't feel and trying to hide his own tension.

He had barely finished the sentence when they heard a deafening noise, like a thousand tree branches pounding against the capsule. Confused images of vegetation appeared in the front window, a sign that they were about to hit the ground. Kal operated the controls, frantically trying to reverse the engine's direction. A few seconds later, the capsule hit something solid and came to a halt.

"I thought you'd never wake up."

Kal opened his eyes and looked up. Amber's voice made it clear that she was in pain. She was still in her seat, breathing heavily.

"Are you okay?" he asked.

"I could be better. I think I cracked a rib or something. It hurts like hell, but otherwise, I'm all right."

Kal sat up and took stock of his own situation. His right knee hurt, and he had a splitting headache, but he seemed to be fine aside from that. A swelling in his head, where he had bumped it on the controls, accounted for his temporary loss of consciousness.

"We're alive, and that's a miracle in itself," he pointed out. "Where are we?"

"I've no idea, except that we crash-landed in a cornfield."

"A cornfield?" Kal had never seen natural corn. He recalled hearing that corn grew all over the planet in the old days and was used as a natural fuel. "Who still grows corn?" he wondered.

"We do, in Freeland. It's tasty and nutritious."

"You eat fuel?" Kal marveled.

"No, stupid. We eat corn. It's good."

"Whatever ..."

Kal got up, testing his joints as he did so, finding no more sore spots.

"Can you stand?" he asked.

"I guess so. Give me a hand."

Kal pulled her gently from the seat, and she stood, one arm pressing against her ribs.

"I'm okay," she said, although the spasms of pain on her face and the beads of perspiration on her brow told a different story.

"I want to see what damage we have and what we can do, but you don't have to come with me; you can wait here and rest," said Kal.

"I prefer to get out of this thing," said Amber, and Kal nodded, lowering the hatch.

Outside, Kal climbed up the side of the capsule to inspect the engine that hung above the cabin. "Birds!" he cried.

"What?"

"That's what happened. I see dead birds inside the engine."

Kal climbed down and stood to face Amber. He had bad news.

"So what can be done?" she asked.

"There's nothing we can do. The engine is ruined, and this capsule can't fly anymore. We're grounded."

"Are you saying that a tiny little bird can bring this flying monster down?"

"First of all, the bird is not so tiny, and there are a whole bunch of them in there. Besides, in The City, you never see any birds, and this engine was not designed to survive them. I'm sorry, I know you're hurting, but we must continue on foot."

"Oh well ..." Amber shrugged.

"I'll get my rucksack, and we'll go."

When he returned, Kal had the pilot's gun attached to his belt. He held the weapon taken from the dead Immaculate out for Amber.

"You'd better keep this," he said. "It may come in handy."

Amber nodded and took it.

The sun was already high in the sky when they reached the edge of the cornfield. They had walked slowly because every step brought a sharp pain to Amber's side. At times, it felt as if they would never find their way out of the corn. As they emerged from the field, a strange vision awaited them: a man sat in a horse carriage, an ancient double-barreled shotgun in his hands. He wore a straw hat and sported a long, white beard above a lean body. At first, Kal thought that he was a statue, so silent and still the man remained as they approached. But then he moved, pointing the gun at them.

"Stay!" he commanded, and Kal and Amber stopped. "What are you doing on my land?"

"We had an accident, sir," Amber said. "We crash-landed, and we are hurt."

"You crash-landed in my corn and ruined quite a bit of it. You need to repay me."

"Can you please lower your gun, sir?" Kal said. "You can see that my companion is hurt and needs help. We will do what we can to repay you for your trouble," he added.

The man remained pensive for a moment, then moved the gun's muzzle away from them. "Okay, you can come," he said, still speaking gruffly.

"Thank you," said Kal and Amber in unison.

"Get up in the back," said the man when they reached the carriage. "I'm Aron," he added.

"I'm Kal, and this is Amber."

"Yeah, get in."

A ten-minute trip on a bumpy road took them to their destination. Amber obviously had a hard time keeping from gasping at every pothole that the wheels hit, but she didn't complain. In front of a green hill stood a house built of stone and wood, surrounded by trees. Aron brought the carriage to a stop outside the front door and turned back to face them.

"Get off," he said, and they complied without commenting.

Aron led the way to the entrance, where he stopped. "Hungry?" he asked.

Kal and Amber hadn't had much time to think about food, but the mere mention of hunger made their bellies rumble.

"In truth," said Kal, "we haven't eaten for a long time, so yes, we're hungry."

"Sit over there," said Aron, pointing to a wooden table on the porch. Then he disappeared inside. When he returned, he had a large loaf of bread, cheese, and some dried meat, which he placed on the table. He went inside again and returned with a carafe of red wine and three glasses.

"Eat," he said, and Kal and Amber didn't need another invitation. They started with the bread and cheese, and soon the dried meat was gone, too. Amber passed on the wine, but Kal drank a little to avoid offending his host. Then, satiated, they lay back in their chairs.

"That was amazing, thank you!" Kal said.

"Can you tell us where we are?" Amber asked.

"You are on my property."

"I understand that," Amber said, "but where is that?"

"It's roughly two hundred miles northeast of Komsk. There's nobody around here for a radius of fifty miles, and I like it that way."

"Don't you get lonely?" Amber asked.

Aron pondered the question for a few seconds before responding.

"I've been on my own for a long time now, ever since my wife died ten ... no, eleven years ago. I don't get many visits, maybe once a year, and most of those I could do without. It's nice seeing young people like you once in a while, though. So what am I going to do with you?"

"What do you mean?" Kal asked, suddenly alarmed.

"I can tell that you're not ordinary people, and I need to know what you're up to. That thing that you were flying in, it's from The City. I don't keep too much track of what goes on over there, but am I right that your uniform is that of an Immaculate?"

"Yes, you're right," Kal conceded.

Aron lifted his double-barreled gun, which he had been holding on his lap, and pointed it at them.

"Wrong answer," he said.

CHAPTER 21

"Now we're in trouble," said Amber testily.

Aron had marched them to a dark basement and had locked them up. Amber's and Kal's attempts to speak to him didn't help.

"Why are you doing this? Please let us explain," Kal had tried to talk to Aron.

"Shut up!" Aron had said.

"Would you please listen to us?" Amber had said.

"Shut up!" Aron had repeated, and that was the end of the conversation.

In the basement, only a little light filtered through a high window.

"He looked like a nice old man," said Amber. "I don't understand what got into him."

"Your 'nice old man' has locked us in his cellar. He took us in and fed us, and I thought we were okay. No doubt he's a little crazy."

They had time to kill; they only didn't know how long it would be.

"Since we don't have anything better to do, tell me what happened at C-54," said Amber.

He told her about Sarah and had to pause when two big tears rolled down her cheeks. After a while, she pulled herself together and demanded to hear more. Kal told her how he came to Komsk, changed clothes, and hid there. He also told her about Dora, or at least the less embarrassing parts of it.

"You're more resourceful than I thought! And this woman, Dora, why did she help you?"

"I think that ... she liked me."

"I sense embarrassment—tell me more!"

"Oh, no, really! Can't we leave it at that? I am embarrassed. I had never been so near a woman before."

"Thank you so much for not counting me as a woman!"

"No, that's not what I meant. Of course, I'm counting on you. But it was different. She was ... how should I say ... familiar."

"Ah, I see," said Amber and stopped asking.

"Now, tell me what happened to you after we got to C-54. I passed out, and the next time I saw you, those Immaculates were taking you to the capsule," said Kal, eager to change the subject.

Amber told him briefly and then clammed up. Kal sat in silence, sensing that she was in a bad mood. After what felt like a long time, the door to the basement opened, and Aron came inside, preceded by his eternal gun.

"So, how did they find me?" he asked.

"How did who find you?" Kal asked, completely nonplussed.

"The Immaculates. Larkin. You didn't deny that your capsule is an Immaculate vehicle and that you are an Immaculate."

"He's not an Immaculate. And, of course, the capsule is an Immaculate vehicle. That's who we stole it from," Amber intervened.

"You stole it? How? Where?"

"It's a long story. I'm not from The City—"

"You're chipless?"

"Yes, I'm—"

"Come over here, but don't try anything foolish. You're covered," Aron said.

Amber hesitated for a moment, but then she walked up to him. Aron gestured for her to turn around, and then he placed his hand on her head and felt her scalp.

Kal opened his mind to the thoughts around him. He had to know what was going on. *They are not City agents. They are not here for me*, was the thought that reached him, and Kal knew that their troubles were, at least temporarily, over.

"You *are* chipless," said Aron. "And what about you?" he asked, turning to Kal.

"He has a chip, but it's damaged," Amber hurried to say. "He's with me; you can trust him."

"We are not City agents. We are not here for you," Kal said, repeating Aron's thoughts.

"I believe you aren't. Sorry for locking you up, but I had to take precautions. I had to go out and see if anybody else was around. I saw no one and heard no other vehicles. I may look like a scarecrow, but I have my equipment, and I know how things work. I checked for electromagnetic activity. If I had found any, it could have meant that other Immaculates were in the area. But I detected none, so I believe you. Come outside. I'll give your stuff back to you. I'll bring something to drink, and we can talk."

He turned and left, followed by Kal and Amber. They again sat at the porch table, and Aron brought a carafe—cider this time—with three glasses. He poured the cider pensively and then took a sip before speaking.

"Let me tell you an interesting tale, but please don't interrupt me until I'm through. Twenty-five years ago, I was an Immaculate. More than that, I was Larkin's second. That was before Larkin went haywire, when we thought we were working for the good of our people. Then I discovered how they were manipulating people. They broadcast what they wanted them to believe and turned everybody into marionettes. I tried to talk to him and then to Alvin, the High Professor, but to no avail. They depend too much on one another. Alvin needs Larkin to do his dirty jobs. Larkin has zero technical capabilities and can't do anything without Alvin. A perfect symbiosis, although in reality, Larkin is the one who calls the shots.

"I reached a point where I could no longer stand it. I started an underground movement to demote Larkin and Alvin, but I underestimated them. Larkin got wind of what I was doing and planned to stage an accident that would leave me dead. I wasn't the only rebel against the system. Others were in it with me, and others were independently rebellious. There were many. The highest-ranking professor who fled The City was someone I would never have suspected of rebellion—"

"Sazar!" Amber cried.

"Yes, Sazar. How did you know?"

"Sazar is my father," Amber said.

"I don't believe it! What are the chances of that?" Aron looked astounded.

"Yes ...," Amber said, turning pensive.

"Sazar's daughter ... incredible," Aron said again, shaking his head. "How did you happen to land on my corn?"

"It's a long story. We had to leave The City because I was chipless. We ended up stealing the capsule, but as you see, it didn't get us far enough. But you were telling me about my father and you back then. I'd like to hear more."

"Well, once your father got away, and some of the people close to me disappeared, I took the hint. I ran away, too, together with my wife. She had relatives who lived here; they were old and tired, so they were happy to have us here to help out. I've been hiding here since. But I know how vindictive Larkin can be. When I saw a City vehicle, I assumed he had kept searching for me and finally tracked me down. I'm glad he didn't. I may have a few more years to live, and I like my life as it is now. I wouldn't want to have to run away again."

"That's an amazing story," said Kal. "So you can help us?"

"Depends on what you need."

"We need to get to Freeland," Amber said before Kal could say anything. "We are going to get married there in one month, and we don't know how to make it in time. It's far away."

Kal gazed at her with surprise but said nothing. He probed her head for a clue to the reason for her lie. She was bright and was putting her thoughts out for him to read. *Play along*, she thought. *I don't trust him. I'll explain later.*

"Oh, good luck!" Aron said. "Sure, I'll help you. But it's more than a thousand miles of bleak LAP land between here and Freeland. Those are dangerous territories inhabited by lawless people. Getting to Freeland without any means of transportation is going to be challenging." He hesitated for a moment and then added, speaking to Kal, "How do you plan to get that chip out of your head? It's not something easy to do without damaging your brain."

"Actually, I haven't given much thought to it. There is no signal where I'm going, so I may as well leave it where it is," said Kal.

"So you don't know ...."

"Don't know what?"

"Sit down, boy. I hate to have to be the one to tell you this. Sit down," he repeated, pointing to a chair. Kal sat down, and Aron went on. "You can't leave The City as you please. Larkin is no fool. Once you have that chip implanted in your head, he owns you forever. There is a self-destruction program in the chip. If it doesn't receive The City signal for twenty-one consecutive days, it self-destructs. When it does, it causes irreparable damage to your brain. I'm sorry."

Kal felt a heavy weight descending on his shoulders. So that was it. Three weeks of freedom and then the end. He opened his mind to probe Aron's thoughts and knew that he was telling the truth.

"Don't worry!" Amber said, speaking emphatically. She placed a reassuring hand on Kal's arm. "As soon as we get to Freeland, they'll take the chip out of your head. Everything is going to be all right."

"*If* we get there on time," Kal said.

"We will. I promise. Trust me."

Aron gazed at Amber and nodded in approval. "Your father must be very proud of you, such a fine young lady."

"Father died a short time ago," Amber lied. Better to lie than to depict herself as someone of potential importance, she thought.

"I'm so sorry," said Aron. "He was a good man."

"Yes, he was," Amber agreed, sadly.

"It's getting late, and it'll be dark soon. Let me show you to your room. You need to rest, young lady. I'll give you something to fixate that rib of yours that I see keeps hurting. Tomorrow we can talk about the future. If you want to shower, it's outside in the back of the house. You need to use the manual pump to fill the tank before you can shower. There's some soap in there, and I can spare a clean towel."

CHAPTER 22

"Kal, I'm scared," Amber whispered.

They both had returned from their respective showers. Kal had gallantly offered his only clean change of clothes to Amber. She looked almost natural in them, but then she had a tomboyish look to start with. Kal had dressed again in his country clothes and was acutely aware of their odor. The room that Aron had assigned to them was on the top floor of the two-story house, reached via a squeaky wooden staircase.

"What about?" he asked.

"Not here," she whispered again.

Kal nodded and pointed at his head, asking if he should try to read her thoughts.

"Let's go out," said Amber, shaking her head. "But first, I need your help with this sticky plaster that Aron gave me. My side hurts like hell, and the plaster may help a little."

She lifted her shirt, exposing her side.

"Ouch!" she said when Kal touched the spot.

"Sorry. It doesn't look too bad. It's a bit blue and green, and I'm sure it hurts, but I hope that you haven't cracked a rib."

"Whatever. Just be quick with it."

Kal applied the sticky plaster as gently as he could. He hoped that he was doing it right, and Amber kept silent and still throughout. She tucked her shirt back into her trousers, and they went downstairs and out. Aron was on the porch.

"How're you doing?" he asked with a friendly smile.

"Great, thank you!" said Amber, smiling back. "You are amazing. The food and shower were the best things that happened to me in a long time. I feel so good that I talked Kal into going out for a stroll. The night is so beautiful!"

"Yeah, nights are nice over here in the summer. Well, you kids have a good time. I'll stay here and have myself a good smoke," he added, waving a pipe that he had in his hand.

Amber locked her arm with Kal's and pulled him impatiently. They walked along the path that went from the door to the fields. Now and then, she turned around to gaze toward the porch. Aron remained sitting there, smoking. At last, Kal stopped.

"We're far enough. He can't hear us. What's eating you?" he asked.

"I'm afraid that Aron may be a ret."

"A what?"

"A ret, a retiree."

"What's that?"

"Don't you know anything? Haven't you heard of the retirees?"

"I don't know what you're talking about."

Amber sighed and shook her head in disbelief.

"I'd better start from the beginning, as Seth explained it to me. After The Pulse, the population—or what remained of it—started getting very sick. New diseases plagued them. A particularly deadly one caused sudden imbalances in blood microelements needed for life. That's when the chip was invented. At first, it was purely a way to follow every citizen's vital signs and blood composition. It gave timely alerts of any dangerous change and of the need to administer treatment. It was a huge health effort that worked quite well."

"I know that, but today the chip can do much more than that for your health. Except, of course, that it can kill you if you're out of line like I am," he added bitterly.

"Yes, but that's only how it was at first. The generation that suffered from The Pulse got old and died, and the new generation no longer suffered from the maladies caused by The Pulse. It wasn't hereditary. As you say, over time, the chip's capabilities evolved and improved to the benefit of the population. The first High Professor invented new methods for loading more powerful software onto the chip, making it more versatile. From there to manipulating the persons implanted with it was a short distance. And then the current High Professor seized power. He was a young, brilliant physicist and had found a way to use the chip to his advantage. At first, it was a study conducted to help people with mental illness, and that's when he and my father worked together. But then Alvin understood the immense power he had in his hands and started to misuse it."

"I didn't know that," said Kal.

"They don't teach you that in school, I guess. Anyway, when that started, it led to a shakeout in the leading scientific layer of government. As you know, only they have access to equipment that lets them turn off their chips—for 'research purposes,' they say. They are in control and cannot be manipulated. Some, like my father, openly rebelled. Many disappeared. Presumably, the High Professor had them killed, but a handful managed to escape. Others chose not to engage in a confrontation with Alvin. Instead, they negotiated an agreement that allowed them to leave The City peacefully. From their exile, they maintained good relations with The City government. Seth estimates that there are about a hundred rets living in various places outside The City. I think that Aron is one of them."

"But why? You saw how scared he was that we might be City agents coming to hunt him down, remember?"

"That could have been an act that he was putting up for us, to make sure that we would feel safe."

"But I read his mind, and he was thinking that we are not City agents and have not come for him," Kal objected.

"Which doesn't mean anything. It may only mean that he was making sure that we were not sent by The City. I don't think that there is full trust between the rets and The City or that there will ever be."

"But why did you start worrying now?"

"I realized something. How long do you think it will take the Immaculates to locate their missing capsule? By now, they must know that something happened."

"With the location equipment they have, I guess that it'll be a matter of hours. I hadn't thought of that!"

"Neither had I, until now ...."

"And Aron must know that he is expecting a visit from the Immaculates, but he enjoys himself on the porch, smoking. My God, you're right!"

"When do you think that Larkin will learn of what we did in Komsk?"

"They may already know it if they have an informant in town. And they must have somebody working for them there; otherwise, how did they know to come and look for you? We must leave immediately!"

Now that he realized the danger, Kal fretted about the little time they probably had before the Immaculates arrived.

"Let's wait a couple of hours and leave as soon as Aron goes to sleep," said Amber.

"We could neutralize him and leave immediately."

"Neutralize him? What, stun him? And what if he is inno-cent?" Amber objected. "He's old and may not withstand a stunning event well. We can't have him on our conscience. But what if he's working with them? Oh, Kal, I'm scared!"

The tension of the last few days had taken a toll on Amber's usual strength. Realizing the danger they were in was too much for her. She started to shake, and Kal pulled her close to him to comfort her. It surprised him that comforting her came so naturally to him.

"We are taking chances by waiting, but you're right, he may be a good person, and I can't harm another in cold blood. I've killed for the first time in my life in self-defense, to save us, but that doesn't make me a killer. Let's do the right thing and get away without harming him."

Amber lifted her head, and their eyes met. "Thank you," she said, and then she kissed him gently. When she stopped, Kal took a deep breath. He had the little experience with Dora to thank for being able to take the kiss without freaking out. He remained composed but was nonetheless surprised.

"What was that for?" he asked with an embarrassed little laugh.

"For saving me and for being a good guy. And to cheer you up. Besides, we must keep up the story of our engagement. Aron hasn't seen us behave as engaged couples should act."

"Yes, I meant to ask you about that story."

"Don't," Amber said, and started walking back to the house.

CHAPTER 23

It was almost midnight, and the house was silent. Loud snoring came from Aron's room next to theirs. Kal and Amber tiptoed out of the room and stopped at the top of the stairs. Kal had his rucksack and held the ray gun in his hand. He motioned for Amber to go down the stairs and stayed at the top, ready to act if Aron came out. Once he saw in the semi-darkness that she had reached the bottom of the stairs, he walked down as well. Amber put two fingers to her temple in a gesture that gave Kal permission to read her mind.

Kal opened his mind to her thoughts. *We need food*, she thought. *I'll go to the kitchen for some.*

Kal nodded to signify understanding and kept watch until she returned holding a sack. They left by the front door and turned toward the stables.

"That's a big sack; what have you got?" Kal asked.

"Bread and cheese and some fruit. Enough to keep us going for a couple of days."

"Great! Let's go inside."

"We can't take the horse," Amber objected. "We don't know

how to harness it or to drive a carriage, and besides, the noise will wake Aron up."

"I know, but if we try to escape on foot and the Immaculates come any time soon, we won't stand a chance. We must try to take the horse."

They opened the door of the stables and tiptoed in. They walked toward the horse, but then Kal stopped.

"Look there! That's the solution," he said with satisfaction.

"What is?"

"A rickshaw. You can sit in it, and I'll pedal. I'll be your horse —one you know how to harness," he added jokingly.

"We'll take turns pedaling. That's much better than the horse. Let's go!"

They pushed the rickshaw out, trying to make as little noise as possible. Once on the road, Amber got in the backseat, and Kal started to pedal. They took the road they had taken to the house and went as far as the first intersection they came to.

"Where to now?" Kal asked.

"If we go right, it's uphill, so it's harder work," said Amber.

"We'll turn right all the same. First, the hills are close. And second, if we need to hide, we have a much better chance of finding a good place than in the plane area. And then if someone comes after us, they will think it more likely that we have turned left."

"You're right," said Amber, "but I want to do my part of the pedaling."

"I'll let you, I promise, but not yet. Your ribs still hurt; I know it, so I'll go first. I'll tell you when I'm tired."

Amber nodded, and Kal turned right, pedaling at an even pace. Soon they reached the hills, and the going got harder. Kal pedaled without speaking, breathing through his nose and trying not to let the effort show too much. It had been more than two hours since they had left Aron's house when Kal brought the rickshaw to a halt.

"We switch?" Amber asked.

"No, listen," said Kal. "In a little while, it will be sunrise. We should hide during the day, at least until we see if the Immaculates are coming after us. Here, to our right, is a nice cove between those two hills, with plenty of vegetation. We should stop here."

"Yes, that makes sense," Amber agreed.

She got off the rickshaw, and together they pushed it off the road and into a patch of grass that led to a shaded area. There, they covered it with fern fronds. When they finished, it was completely invisible from the road. Then they continued on foot toward the place where the two hills met.

"Do you hear that?" Amber asked.

"Yes, it's running water. That explains this much vegetation."

A creek ran not far away from where they had stopped. Broad-leafed trees provided shade and cover from anything that might fly above them. They drank avidly and then sat down, their backs to a large tree. The first light was already on the horizon.

"We should catch up on our sleep a little, don't you think?" said Amber.

"I'm asleep already," Kal said, smiling.

When they woke up, the sun was high in the sky. Its rays passed through the branches of the tree above them, illuminating the scene. But it wasn't the sun that had woken them up.

"What's that?" Amber asked, shaking away the mists of sleep.

"Immaculates!" said Kal.

The pulsating sound of an engine was almost overhead. Looking through the foliage, they saw a capsule flying low over the hills. They watched as it flew back and forth. At times, it seemed about to land on them. Finally, it disappeared in the distance.

"It's gone," said Kal.

"What time is it?"

"Almost noon, by the position of the sun."

"You were right; we can't be out in the open in broad daylight. They would have seen us in a second."

"That's dangerous. We'll have to stay here until dark. I don't think that they'll keep looking for long. If they can't find us, they'll give up after a while, but we need a plan. We can't keep running away aimlessly. Time is running out for me, and we must plan how to get to Freeland."

"First of all, we must eat," said Amber, pulling the food sack toward her. "I'm starved."

They ate and drank water from the creek, and then they sat down to plan ahead. Kal took the map that Seth had given him and unfolded it on the grass.

"If I'm reading this right, we are more or less here," he said, pointing to a place on the map. "The question is how we get from here to Freeland."

"I never made a real plan for it. My idea was childish, I guess. I thought that once I got my father out of The City, we would go to the C-54 travel lodge. Then Adam would contact Afex, who would send an air vehicle to pick us up from there. When Seth asked me to guide you, I thought I would do the same. How stupid of me!"

"Don't be too hard on yourself. It could have worked under different circumstances."

"The problem is that circumstances are never different," said Amber, speaking bitterly. "Now we'll have to travel the LAP land to get to Freeland. It's a lawless land. They taught me in school that LAP people are greedy. Entire populations have disappeared or changed for the worse as a result of The Pulse that had its epicenter there. It's a horrible land, and we have to cross it."

"Don't worry, we'll be fine," said Kal, in a transparent attempt to console her.

"Yeah ... how are we going to pass the time until night?" she asked in a sudden change of subject.

"We can rest," Kal suggested.

"Or, instead, we can do something useful. Once we leave the Surroundings, we may get into all kinds of problems. You may have to use your telepathic gift to get us out of trouble, so we would be smart to exercise beforehand."

"How?"

"Let's see if I can get you to understand what I'm trying to say, using quick mental images. Close your eyes, and when I tell you, try to read me."

They lay on the grass, side by side, and Kal closed his eyes.

"Now," Amber said.

"Uhmm, you want us to get out. Out of what?"

"Concentrate."

"A door—yes, we are in a building, and you want us to leave."

"Yes, but it took you too long to get it. Let's keep trying."

They exercised for almost an hour until Amber finally declared herself satisfied.

"Okay, now you get me every time, and you're fast enough. That should do."

"Good. I was starting to get tired. You are difficult to please," Kal said, laughing.

"I know I am. I have always been demanding, way too much so. I have been too hard on myself, getting ready for my mission. How naïve that was, thinking that I could come to The City and rescue my father single-handedly. I feel a little stupid now."

"That's not stupid. I think you are very brave."

"Do you? Being so purpose-driven, I missed so much. All my friends had fun, developed relationships, and *lived*. Now, if we can't make it back, I may never have that. I may die a stupid, young girl who experienced nothing in her life."

"Oh, don't say that! First of all, we'll make it. I promise. And you are getting much more out of life now than you did from meaningless teenage fun. You have a purpose, and that's a huge thing. In The City, teenagers spend their time learning and improving. They don't waste time and energy engaging in irresponsible behavior."

"But aren't you sorry that you missed that? Now that you know what life is like outside The City? I bet that woman, Dora, made you regret the lost time ...."

Kal knew better than to bring Dora into the discussion.

"Not at all. I'm happy about the way I grew up. There is serenity in living in a society where human relations are predictable and smooth. You don't have to guess what's going to happen next. But you—you can make up for lost time any way you want."

Amber smiled and said nothing for a minute. She gazed up at the sky between the tree branches, and then she turned her head toward him.

"You are sweet, trying to encourage me like that; thank you," she said. "Can you figure out what I'm thinking now?"

"One more exercise? Do you want me to read you?"

"Yes," she said and closed her eyes.

Kal opened his mind to her thoughts and remained silent for a few seconds.

"Really?" he said, at last, speaking almost in a whisper.

"Uh-huh," she said, without opening her eyes.

Kal's heart was racing at a rate that his H-cubicle would have found abnormal. It was all very confusing to him, but he realized that he wanted to follow her lead, wherever that would take him. He propped himself up on his elbow and leaned toward her. Moving slowly, he brought his lips to hers and touched them. When her lips parted in response, he kissed her gently. He realized that he had wanted to do it since she had kissed him outside Aron's house.

"That's enough," Amber said, pushing him away.

"Why? What?"

"I was doing a little catching up. Like you said. I'm done for now."

She turned on her side with her back to Kal. Kal was left to ruminate on how little he understood girls and their erratic behavior.

CHAPTER 24

Amber applied the brakes to the rickshaw and stopped.

"Tired?" Kal inquired. He had let her pedal for the last half hour because she had become insistent. But sitting in the backseat and letting her do the work felt wrong.

"No, but this is it. This is where we ditch the rickshaw. Over that ridge, there is the border into LAP land, and it's too steep to climb with the rickshaw."

"Let me see," said Kal, getting out of the rickshaw and spreading the map on the seat. "You're right," he said after studying it for a little while. "And you see here," he added, pointing to a point on the map, "it says that this is a travel lodge. It must be no more than five miles from here, and if we're lucky, it will be up and running."

"It'd better be," said Amber. "It will be daylight in three hours, and we need someplace to stay. It's all flat land over the ridge and no vegetation, so there's nowhere to hide in the open."

"It looks like they've given up looking for us. We haven't heard them for a full day now."

"I hope so, too, but do you want to gamble on that?"

Kal left the question hanging. He turned his attention to finding a place to hide the rickshaw. The ruins of a small building off the road looked like a perfect hiding place, and he pushed the rickshaw into it. Unless somebody actually walked into the ruined building, it would be hidden from view. Returning to the road, he joined a pensive Amber.

"A penny for your thoughts," he joked.

"You can have them for free—you know that."

"And you know that I will never read you unless I have permission. Besides, I prefer to hear your voice."

"I was thinking of the long way that is ahead of us."

"I'd rather not think about it. Are we going?"

They climbed the steep road to the top of the ridge. Then they navigated the equally steep descent into the plane ahead. They walked for almost three hours before they saw a faint light shining in the distance.

"That light must be the travel lodge, and it means that it's open. That's good," said Kal.

They walked in silence, too tired to talk. When they reached the travel lodge, the sun was already rising, and a man was outside, brushing a horse. On seeing them, he stopped his brushing and waited for them to approach.

"Howdy!" he said when they were close enough to hear.

"Hi!" Kal answered, trying to sound casual. "Are you open for business?"

"We sure are," said the man.

He was short, with blond hair and a short, blond beard that made him look well-groomed. He looked a little younger than forty and wore a red-and-blue checkered shirt over blue jeans. Despite his welcoming attitude, his hand was on the grip of an old-fashioned firearm that hung from his belt.

"Where did you sprout up from?" he asked with a smile.

"We came from the Surroundings," said Amber.

"I can guess that seeing the direction you're coming from, but there is nothing for twenty miles around here. That's quite a hike that you've been doing."

"Do you have a room? And breakfast?" Kal asked, anxious to steer the conversation away from them.

"Do you have money?" retorted the man.

"How much?"

"One piece of silver and five bronze for the room and veggie breakfast. Two pieces if you want meat as well."

"That's too expensive ..." Amber said.

"We haven't had a proper meal lately ...," Kal said, leaving it hanging.

"Listen," said the man, "come inside and sit down. I was making coffee. I'll fetch you some, and in the meantime, you can make up your mind. I am John, by the way, the owner."

Inside, the room was small, with four square tables. At the closest one, a man sat bent over a glass of liquor. His hair and long beard were unkempt, and his clothes were greasy. He looked like a hobo. He eyed them and then went back to looking at his glass. Kal pulled Amber toward the table farthest away from him. "He stinks," he whispered.

"So, what will it be?" John asked once they were seated.

"We'll tell you in a moment," Kal said.

"I'll be back," said John.

"We need to eat properly," Kal said to Amber after John left.

"Sure. I want it too. I was just putting on an act for our host, so he doesn't think that we are rich."

"Very shrewd of you," said Kal, smiling.

John came back with a pot and two cups and poured coffee.

"Have you made up your minds?" he asked.

"We'll take the meat," said Kal.

"Wise choice. If you throw in three more bronze pieces, you can keep the room until tomorrow at noon."

"Okay," Kal agreed.

"You pay in advance here. House rule."

Kal fished the purse from his rucksack, counted out the money, and handed it to him. John left and returned with a succulent breakfast tray with eggs, meat, bread, and potatoes. Kal and Amber ate everything on the tray and drank the coffee to the last drop. They ate in silence, and the unkempt man shot them glances every now and then over his glass. When all the food was gone, Kal waved to John.

"Breakfast was delicious, thank you. Now we'd like to get some rest."

"You have weapons, right?"

"How do you know?"

"You don't look like fools to me, and only fools travel these lands without weapons. But you can't keep them. House rule. I'll lock them in a safety box, and you'll get one of the keys. I'll give them back to you when you leave."

"You seem to have a lot of house rules," said Amber.

"You ain't heard nothing yet," John said with a smile.

They followed him to the office, where they locked both their guns away. John handed them one of the two keys needed to open the safety box. Then he led them up a short staircase to a bare room except for a large, low bed, a chest of drawers, and an empty closet.

"There is no running water here," said John. "If you need water, the pump is at the back of the house. The toilet is outside, and you'll recognize it by the smell," he added with a crooked smile. "If you need anything during the day, come down. I'll be in the dining room or the kitchen if I'm not outside tending to my horse. Questions?"

Kal shook his head. He felt too tired to speak, and all he wanted was to see the man go so that he could crash on the bed. John left, closing the door behind him, and Amber and Kal took off their shoes and lay side by side on the bed.

"You said that the man downstairs stunk, didn't you?" Amber said, speaking drowsily.

"Yes …"

"I just got a whiff of you. No perfume, either."

"Sorry about that. Remind me when we get up," Kal said with a little laugh. He turned to one side and closed his eyes.

———— · —— · ————

Judging by the sun that was high in the sky, it was noon when Kal woke up. Amber was up, gazing out the window, and she turned to him when she heard him move.

"Good morning," said Kal.

"I've been awake for an hour already, and I'm fresh out of the shower. Not a great experience, but I'm a new girl. Get up and go take one, too."

"In a minute. Let me wake up. I'm not sure I'm awake yet. I'm dying to sleep a little longer."

"You can sleep tonight. Traveling by night here is not safe, right? And if we don't see any Immaculate vehicle searching for us by the end of the day, it's safe to assume that they have given up."

"You're right. Let's spend the night here and leave first thing tomorrow morning."

"Go take a shower, and then we need to eat. I'm famished!"

———— · —— · ————

Lunch and dinner put another dent in their purse, but they didn't mind. John's cuisine was fabulous, and they enjoyed the break and the rest in a real bed. They had an early dinner and went to sleep so they would be ready to leave early the following day.

They had been asleep for a couple of hours when Kal woke up with a jerk. Something was wrong. A foul smell reached his nostrils, and he opened his eyes. The hobo was in the room and was holding a knife to Amber's throat.

"Your purse," he said curtly. "Move, or I cut her."

Amber's eyes were wide open, and Kal saw fear in them.

"Don't do anything stupid," he said, speaking quietly for fear of provoking him. "I'll give you the money."

He reached for his rucksack and fished into it, pulling out the purse. He held it in front of him, and the hobo snatched it and stuffed it into his pocket. With the knife still on Amber's throat, he retreated toward the door.

"Stay where you are," he ordered.

Once he reached the door, walking backward, he pushed Amber away so hard that she fell to the floor, and he fled. Kal jumped up and started to go after him, but Amber's voice stopped him.

"No, don't!" she cried.

"He took all our money. We are left with nothing. I must get it back," Kal said, speaking urgently.

"He has a knife. He'll kill you. It isn't worth it. Don't go," she pleaded.

Resigned to losing his purse, Kal offered her his hand and pulled her up. She hugged him and pushed her head into his shoulder, shaking.

"That's all right. Cry it out," said Kal.

"I'm not crying," she said, sniffing.

"Whatever you say," said Kal.

He kept her close until she stopped shaking, and then they sat side by side on the bed.

"What are we going to do?" she asked at last.

"We'll manage somehow," he comforted her. "Let's try to get some sleep, at least."

"Block the door. I can't sleep like this."

The only furniture in the room was a chest of drawers, and Kal dragged it against the door.

"Here," he said. "If anybody tries to get in, we will hear him."

They lay on the bed for a while, gazing at the ceiling.

"Hold me," Amber said at last.

"I stink," said Kal, trying to lighten up the atmosphere.

"I don't care," she said.

He got closer and held her until they both, exhausted as they were, fell asleep again.

———

"How was your night?" John inquired, smiling, as they came down the stairs into the dining room.

"We were mugged!" said Kal, speaking pointedly. The owner must have had something to do with what happened, he reasoned.

"You don't say," said the owner, lifting an eyebrow. "When?"

"Last night. Here in your place. Who's that hobo? The one who was here when we arrived."

"Listen, mister. I had nothing to do with it. If you didn't look after yourself, that's your problem. This is a travel lodge, not a kindergarten. I don't know much about that hobo, either. He lives up in the hills and comes here every few weeks to drink himself up until he rolls over on the floor. He's no friend of mine, only a customer. If you have a bone to pick with him, go up the hills to find him and have it out, but don't come whining to me."

"He took all our money," said Amber in a low voice.

"Well, then, how do you plan to pay for your breakfast?"

"I don't know," said Kal in despair. "And we also need some food for the road."

"I'll tell you what I'll do. I'm doing this only because I like you, and I feel generous today. I'll take one of those two guns as payment for breakfast and supplies for the road. What do you say?"

"A gun like that is worth much more than some food!" said Amber. "What about adding three pieces of silver?"

"You're kidding, right? I don't need your gun. I'm doing you a favor. If you don't want it, that's your decision."

"We'll give you one of the guns," said Kal.

Amber and Kal ate moodily but finished everything that John brought them. Then they picked up their stuff, one of the two guns, and the small basket of food that John had prepared and left without saying goodbye.

CHAPTER 25

"This is where you get off," the old farmer said.

The carriage made an abrupt stop when the horse tardily realized that the reins were being pulled. Kal and Amber jumped down from the conductor's seat, where they had traveled beside the old man.

"I don't know how to thank you," said Kal. "That would have been a long trip on foot."

The old man spat a long brown stream of chewing tobacco. "No sweat," he said. "I was going this way. If you follow this road, you'll be in town in fifteen minutes."

"Thanks again," said Amber.

"Uh-huh," said the old man. "Watch your girl down there. These are bad times, and bad people come to these parts," he added, looking Kal straight in the eyes. He touched the horse with his whip, and the carriage moved.

"Wow, isn't he gloomy!" said Amber.

"I'm afraid he knows what he's talking about. Anyway, he was God-sent. The three-hour ride we had with him would've taken us all day on foot. Thank God we're only a few minutes away from town."

"You seem to be thanking God a lot. Do you remember that we are going to walk into town without any money? What are we going to do when we get there?"

"We'll manage. We'll think of something."

"Like what?"

"We'll manage," Kal insisted and started walking.

It was already late afternoon, and the air was cool, making the hike easy and almost pleasant. Soon, the outskirts of the town came into view, and then they reached the first houses.

"Look, they're having a fair," said Kal, pointing to a large sign that said "Resurrection Spring Fair—All-New Attractions, Lotteries, and Prizes."

"Resurrection—what a name to pick for a town," said Amber.

"Quite apt; look here," said Kal.

A large sign told the story of the town.

Resurrection arose on the ashes of a once-thriving city, it said. *Close to a million souls disappeared on the night of The Pulse, leaving empty buildings, houses, and streets. Where a dynamic community once existed, only silence remained. Survivors from all over this great area came into town, searching its crumbling buildings for signs of life, for relatives, friends, and acquaintances, and finding none. They turned over a new leaf in an old town with a new name, vowing to forget the way of life that existed before The Pulse in favor of a new, better one. Resurrection was founded so that those who were here before us should not be forgotten, and their memory lives in the essential resurrection of our life.*

Dedicated by the Town Council on the 50th anniversary of The Pulse.

"Brrr. It doesn't get more depressing than that," said Amber.

"By the sound of it, there is some merrymaking going on."

Music reached them from between the houses, and they followed it. Turning a corner, they came upon a large square filled with stalls that sold all kinds of merchandise. The evening was creeping in, and more people seemed to be arriving every minute.

Nobody paid attention to them as they wandered about. At the edge of the square, a large crowd had assembled around an elevated platform. A man was shouting from it at the top of his voice, "All bets are open. Come see the daring devil who is going to play with our champion. I am your humble master of ceremonies, and my colleague here, our bookie, will take your bets. Come, gents. It's almost time!"

"Let's see what the commotion is about," said Kal. He grabbed Amber's hand and pulled her through the crowd until they reached the platform.

"Let me remind you of the rules. This is all fair and square—don't let anybody say otherwise. Our champion here has three knives. Cheers for the champion!" he shouted.

He approached a big man who stood at the end of the platform, took his hand, and raised it, prompting applause and shouts from the crowd.

"And here is our contender—what's your name again?" he asked. The contender was a small man, about twenty-five years old, who stood shirtless at the other end of the platform, some thirty feet from the champion. "James? Okay, our contender is James. Give James a big hand; he deserves it!"

The crowd applauded and whistled loudly. When the shouts stopped, the master of ceremonies continued his exposition.

"The rules are simple. Our champion will throw three times. He can throw center, left, or right. Our contender must guess where the champion has chosen to throw, then move to the other side. If he is mistaken or too slow, our champion's knife will strike him. If he guesses right three times, his reward will be all the money of the losing bets, but no less than fifty silver coins. If he's hit but remains alive, his share will be one-third of the losing bets. You can bet on success, one nonfatal hit, two nonfatal hits, three nonfatal hits—very uncommon—or death. Start betting. We begin in five minutes!"

The crowd started betting with frenzy as Kal and Amber

watched, amazed. Five minutes later, the master of ceremony climbed on the platform again and raised his hands.

"All bets off. We begin!" he declared.

Silence descended on the crowd as they watched the two men on the platform getting ready to start. James, the contender, took a position at the center of the wooden wall erected at his end of the platform. The champion took his first knife and caressed its blade thoughtfully. The master of ceremonies took his position in a corner next to the champion.

"Begin!" he cried.

The champion went into a throwing position, the blade raised in his right hand. He stood there, frozen except for his head, which moved from side to side. Suddenly, his hand went forward, and he threw the blade. James jumped to his right side, and the blade missed him and got stuck in the wall. Thunderous applause came from the crowd, and Kal found himself applauding, too.

"Next!" the master of ceremonies called out.

The champion repeated his performance, only this time James chose to jump to the wrong side. The blade found his throat, sending him to the ground, where he bled to death. The crowd went wild with shouts and applause, and those who had bet right went to collect their winnings. Two helpers jumped onto the platform and removed James's body. A third came up with a bucket of water and washed the blood away. In under three minutes, any sign that James had ever existed was erased. The master of ceremonies again climbed onto the platform and raised his hands.

"Gentlemen, gentlemen," he cried, to quiet the crowd, "I know you're having a good time, and those of you who bet right got value for their money, but we want to go on. So now I'm calling for a new contender. Who thinks he can outsmart our champion? The stakes are high—this time, the losing bets are for more than three hundred silver pieces. That's a lot of money if you have the guts to take a chance and if you think you're smart and fast. So who's going to be our next contender? Come on, we're waiting!"

"I am!" Kal cried, raising his hand.

"Are you out of your mind?" Amber hissed to him, turning pale.

"I'm not, don't worry."

"Don't worry? *Don't worry?* You're crazy!"

"No, I know what I'm doing. We need this money if we want to get to Freeland before the chip blows my brain up. Believe me, I'll win."

"Are you coming or not?" asked the master of ceremonies impatiently.

"I'm coming," said Kal, freeing himself from Amber's grasp. He handed her his rucksack and climbed onto the platform.

"Who do we have here? What's your name, young man?"

"I'm Orlo," Kal lied.

"Orlo, good. Please give Orlo a big hand. He has courage and deserves it. This will be our last game of the day, so bet well and bet heavily. This is your chance to make a big win!" he cried.

The betting went on in an even greater frenzy than before. It took ten minutes before the master of ceremonies climbed onto the platform and again gave his "all bets off" cry. Silence fell on the crowd as Kal took a position against the wall. The champion repeated his concentration routine and threw. When his hand moved forward, Kal jumped to his right, and the knife sank into the wooden wall. The crowd applauded, but only half-heartedly. They were obviously disappointed that they weren't seeing blood.

With the second throw, Kal jumped to his right again, and the knife hit the wall. On the third throw, Kal remained still, and the blade hit the wall to his right. The crowd went wild with applause. The knife-throwing champion hurried down from the platform with a dazed expression on his face. The master of ceremonies obviously decided to put a good face on his bad luck and jumped onto the platform. He took Kal's hand and raised it, declaring, "The winnah!"

"Gentlemen!" he continued, "this young man has done the unimaginable. He has beaten our champion three times. Three times!" he repeated, getting an even louder round of applause. "Now you deserve your win—sixty-three silver coins, congratulations!"

He handed Kal a purse, and when Kal failed to take it, the crowd went silent, sensing that something was about to happen.

"My win is four hundred forty-seven silver pieces. I want them all," Kal whispered in a low voice that the crowd could not hear.

"What? Are you crazy?" the master of ceremonies whispered back.

"What's going on? Speak up!" someone shouted from the crowd.

Kal turned toward the crowd. "This man is trying to cheat me out of my prize," he said out loud. "He owes me four hundred forty-seven silver pieces, not sixty-three. I put it to you—haven't I earned it?"

Cries of "Yes!" and "Pay him!" came from the crowd. An elderly man made his way to the platform, pushing everybody in his way aside with authority.

"Leave this to me, boy," he said, "I'm the mayor. You give him his money, mister, understood?" he added, addressing the master of ceremonies, "or you'll end up in prison. We don't condone thieves in this town. This boy must get his win."

With an ashen face, the master of ceremonies counted out the correct amount. He handed it to Kal, and then he stepped down from the platform and disappeared. Kal approached the mayor.

"Thank you, sir," he said.

"That's all right, boy. We have no patience for swindlers in Resurrection," said the mayor. He grabbed Kal's hand and shook it. "You sure have guts," he added appreciatively. "Now go and celebrate."

The crowd had already dwindled, and Kal made his way to where Amber was standing.

"I hate you!" she whispered to him.

"Why? I won us a lot of money."

"I thought I'd die every time he threw that blade."

"But I told you that I knew what I was doing. I was reading his mind, and I knew exactly what he was about to do and when."

"You could have missed," she said accusingly.

"I don't think so, but that's a chance that I had to take. I read the mind of the bookkeeper, and I knew that the stakes were high."

The light on the platform had gone off, and the few people who still gathered near it in small groups were discussing the events. A few were talking about Kal. A woman smiled at him invitingly, and he ignored her.

"Keep your voice down," Amber admonished him. "You already took a big chance saying the right sum out loud. Lucky that people were so dazzled that you didn't get killed, that nobody thought of asking how you knew it."

"Yes, that was a mistake, but I had to demand my money. What's so funny?" he asked when Amber gave a sudden laugh.

"You. The mayor. 'We don't condone thieves in this town,'" she parroted him. "I was thinking how he would react if he knew that *you* were cheating."

"Aren't you hungry?" Kal asked, changing the subject.

"Starving."

"Let's go and find a good place to eat. We're rich!" Kal said with a broad smile.

CHAPTER 26

K al leaned back with a satisfied sigh. The restaurant that a passerby had recommended to them had more than met their expectations.

"That was tasty," he said, and Amber nodded in assent.

"I needed that," she agreed. "Now we have to find someplace to stay the night."

"Before we attend to that, I want to speak to that man at that corner table," said Kal, pointing his chin toward the table. Three men sat there, eating in silence.

"Why? Who's that?"

"Aha! While you were busy stuffing yourself with food, I was working. I made a round of the room, reading people and searching for useful information. That man over there—the one with the red beard—is organizing a convoy of goods to Freeland. We want to be with that convoy."

"That's amazing! You're amazing! What luck!"

"Yes, but we need to make him take us first. He's transporting goods, not passengers."

"In this place, money can buy you anything."

"I hope so. Let's go and talk to him."

They approached the table and waited for the red-bearded man to finish speaking with the man seated beside him. Sensing their presence, he gazed up and took a long look at Kal and Amber.

"D'you wan' somph'n?" he asked.

"Yes, sir. We hear that you are leading a convoy to Freeland."

"Who told you that?"

"I asked around. Someone said that you are. I don't know his name. Isn't that right?"

"It's right enough, but what is it to you?"

"We—my fiancée and I—we must get to Freeland to get married and are looking to join a convoy that goes there."

"Boy, you can get a priest here for two cents and get married today. Traveling this land to get to Freeland is no pleasure trip. It's not for you. Now, if you don't mind, my friends and I here are busy."

The man turned around, indicating that the matter was closed. But the one sitting at his right whispered something in his ear, and he turned to Kal again.

"Is it right what my friend here says that you're the boy who won the knife-throwing competition today?"

"Yes, that's me."

"That makes a difference. My convoy is no place for softies, but you are gutsy. And you made a bundle and can pay, right?"

"We can pay for a place in your convoy, yes," said Kal.

"Fifty silver pieces a head. Now," said the man.

"And you'll take us as far as—?"

"The goods exchange station with Freeland," said the man.

"It's okay," Amber said in an undertone, "that's half a day's travel from where I live. That'll do fine."

"All right then," said Kal.

He took out his purse and counted a hundred silver pieces in fives and tens. The man watched as he counted, took the money, and then nodded in approval.

"My name is Lorenson. You'll find me at the goods depot at

the northern edge of town. Everybody here knows where that is—day after tomorrow. We leave at six in the morning. If you're late, you'll be left behind, so be there on time. I'll fix you up with one of the trucks. Expect no luxury because you won't get none. Be thankful that you have wheels that will take you to your destination, and don't come bitching to me about travel conditions. I ain't listening. No refunds, by the way."

"One more question. We are new in town. Can you recommend a good place to stay?"

"The Cinder Hotel, across the street and two blocks on the right, is the best, but it's always pretty busy. If they have rooms, you're lucky. The place is clean, and they won't rip you off. Now get the hell away from my table and let me finish my meal in peace."

Kal thanked him, and they returned to their table.

"Finding a convoy to Freeland is a lucky strike," said Amber. "A convoy of goods may attract robbers, but on the flip side, it is sure to be well guarded. It is certainly safer than trying to make it on our own."

"I agree," said Kal, getting up. "Wait for me here for a few minutes. I want to go and see this hotel and try to get a room. I'll leave the bag here with you and will be back in no time."

"I could come with you."

"No point. I'll check the place out and get a room if one is available, and if not, I'll try to find something else. It'll be quicker if I do this alone, and I don't want to walk around with all the money before I know where we are going. I'll leave the purse in the rucksack."

Amber nodded. She was so tired that she didn't insist. In fact, she suspected that Kal wanted to spare her the trouble and let her rest. She took their rucksack, dragged it under her feet, and closed her eyes to rest a little.

Kal left the eatery and turned right as Lorenson had explained.

He reached the corner of the building and stopped for a moment to look for a sign to the hotel. That was when someone grabbed him from behind. A sack descended over his head, and then everything went black.

CHAPTER 27

Amber knew that something was wrong. Kal had been gone for more than one hour. At first, she had closed her eyes and dozed off a little, but now she was worried sick and didn't know what to do. Remaining in the restaurant was safer than walking the streets of that strange town with all that money on her. But staying there would not help her to find out what had happened to Kal. He had been away too long for her to think that he was coming back.

The street outside was dark, and she walked toward the hotel. She let out a sigh of relief when she saw an illuminated sign that read "Cinder." The lobby was in semi-darkness. As she entered, the bell on the door let out a raucous ring that suited the room's gloomy appearance. An old woman stepped out from behind a curtain and waited at the reception desk for Amber to approach.

"Good evening," she said. She raised an eyebrow as if to inquire what this was all about.

"Good evening, ma'am," said Amber. "I am looking for my fiancée, who came here to find us a room."

"Nobody's been here all night," said the woman.

"Are you sure? He came over about one hour ago."

"I'm sure. I've been here all the time."

Amber's heart fell. Something had happened to Kal to keep him from getting to the hotel, and she had to think about what to do. She forced herself to act normally without betraying her anxiety. One never knew what a display of emotions could bring.

"Then he must have decided to go on another errand first. Well, now I'm here. Do you have a room for two nights?"

"Do you have money? This is not some cheap hostel, you know."

"I can pay for the room. How much is it?"

"Two pieces of silver per night."

"Let me see the room, and if I like it, I'll pay you for both nights."

The woman now seemed mollified, knowing that she had a paying customer. She managed something resembling a smile and took a key from an almost empty row of hooks behind her.

"Come, and I'll show you," she said.

Amber climbed two flights of stairs behind the woman, and they reached a door in a dark corridor. The room was spacious, with a window looking out to the main street.

"This is one of our best rooms, with an adjoining bathroom, running water, and a shower. You won't find many rooms like this in this town."

"Yes, it'll do. I'll take it," said Amber. "Give me a few minutes to get organized, and I'll come down to pay."

The woman nodded in assent and left. Amber seated herself heavily on the bed and rested her head in her hands. She could finally allow herself to cry and let out all her fear and the tension she had had to deal with during the last few days. She felt so overwhelmed by the situation that she needed a good cry. She also felt guilty because she hadn't insisted that she and Kal should stay together. She had let her fatigue dictate rather than use her common sense. Now she had to cling to the hope that nothing too bad had happened to him and that he would come to the hotel soon and find her. Otherwise, she didn't know what she would do.

———— · ——— · ————

Kal's head hurt. His hands and back hurt, too, and he realized that he was tied to a wooden chair. He was in some kind of basement. Only a little light came through a street-level barred window, allowing him to see that the room was bare. He couldn't remember much of what had happened since that hood had covered his view. He had been thrown into a carriage; he remembered that much. Then someone had carried him downstairs, and he had received a few blows to different parts of his body. He didn't know how long he had been unconscious, but it was still night so that it couldn't be too long.

A door that he hadn't noticed before squeaked open, and two men walked into the basement. One was the master of ceremonies, and the other the knife-thrower. Kal immediately realized that he was in worse trouble than he had imagined. Those people were not simple robbers—they had a grudge against him. And if they chose to keep him as a prisoner, he would die anyway. The chip would kill him. Whichever way it went, he was bound to lose.

"You're awake—good!" said the master of ceremonies. He dragged a chair over and sat on it, facing Kal. "I need two things from you, and then maybe I'll let you live. First of all, my money. It wasn't on you. Where is it?"

"I don't have it anymore. I owed it, and I paid my debt with it," Kal lied.

"Listen to me. I have no patience with your lies. Do you know what this is?" said the master of ceremonies. He pulled a gun from his pocket and showed it to Kal. It was an old firearm, but he knew how deadly it could be.

"I bet you do," the master of ceremonies continued without waiting for an answer. "We'll get back to the money, but first things first. I need to know how you managed to win. We've done this a hundred times, and nobody ever managed to avoid the blade. I want to know how you did it."

Kal realized that if he wanted a chance to stay alive, he had to be smart. He closed his eyes and concentrated on the knife thrower, who observed the scene with little interest. *I do all the hard work, and then he'll take all the money like he did last week*, he was thinking. That was something to work on.

"Answer me!" cried the master of ceremonies, slapping Kal hard.

His breath was foul, and it added to Kal's discomfort from being tied and beaten up. He needed a little more time to gather information.

"I don't understand what you want me to say," he said.

"You know what I want. You can't win at my game; people never do. I need to know how you did it."

"All right, I'll tell you. It was Sam's idea."

"Sam's? Who's Sam?"

"Your Sam. Him. The knife thrower."

"Are you mad?" cried the knife thrower. "I've never seen you before in my life."

The master of ceremonies jumped up and took two steps back. He pointed his gun in the direction of the knife thrower.

"Shut up!" he said. "Let him speak."

"He isn't happy about the distribution of the money. You weren't fair to him last week."

"He's crazy!" the knife thrower yelled. "I don't know what he's talking about."

Primed by Kal's words, the knife thrower's thoughts went back to the previous week. He couldn't help it, and that was what Kal needed. He went on, ignoring the knife thrower and addressing the master of ceremonies.

"He approached me and told me that he was fed up with you taking all the profit and letting him do all the hard work. He said that last week you only gave him half his share because he was tired and refused to do another show on the same day."

"He's lying! I never spoke with him," the knife thrower cried.

"Yeah? So how does he know what you and I said to each other, huh? Explain that!"

The master of ceremonies' gun now pointed straight at the knife thrower, and his anger was mounting so much that his voice shook.

"After all I've done for you. After I've taken you from the shit-hole where you lived and given you a good life, that's how you repay me! And I can find a thousand knife throwers better than you. Perhaps you don't see that."

The master of ceremonies was now shaking with rage, and the finger he kept on the trigger had grown white. In a flash, the knife thrower's hand came forward, and a knife flew toward his master. The knife found its mark in the master of ceremony's left shoulder. At the same time, the loud report of a shot and a flash of light marked the gun's discharge. A hole gaped in the knife thrower's brow, and he fell to the ground, bleeding profusely. The master of ceremonies fell to his knees with a cry of pain and dropped the gun. After a few seconds, he straightened himself up and pulled the knife from his shoulder. He bled copiously and was obviously in great pain. He tore away his left sleeve with his good hand and used it as a bandage to stop the bleeding. Kal all the while watched, reading the man's confused thoughts. *I need a doctor ... the money can wait for later ... God, that hurts!*

The master of ceremonies finished bandaging himself as best as he could. He picked up the gun and faced Kal.

"I've got to have this fixed, but I'll be back, and if you don't give me back my money, I'll leave you here to rot with this traitor. Understand?"

Without waiting for an answer, he left, and Kal heard a key turn in the lock. Light came through the narrow window and told him that it was already morning. The sounds from outside were those of a town waking up. With nothing else to do, he tried to read the thoughts of people passing in the street outside. Those were few and far between, but perhaps he would learn where he was being held, which would help him somehow.

───────

Amber hadn't been able to sleep. In fact, she hadn't tried, but she had dozed off at intervals, overcome by fatigue. She got up as the first rays of the morning sun found their way into the room. She undressed and went into the shower. It had been a long time since she had enjoyed the luxury of a proper indoor shower, and she lingered in it. After a while, she felt ashamed that she was enjoying it and hurried out. With Kal who knew in what danger, enjoying anything felt wrong. She dried herself off and dressed. She had to go out and do ... she didn't know exactly what, but something. She hid the rucksack with the money and the gun under the bed, locked the door, and took the key with her. She left stealthily, hoping that the hotel staff would think that she was still in her room. She didn't feel safe walking around with the purse or the gun.

Once in the street, she had to decide which way to go. Wherever Kal was, he was not in plain sight, so she had to be out there, hoping that he would see her. It was a faint hope, but she didn't have a better plan. She decided to go back to the restaurant and, from there, to retrace Kal's movements toward the hotel. She would walk for a while, then return via a parallel street, and in that way she would comb the town. It wasn't a big town, and its downtown area was small. But Kal could be miles away by that time. Still, she had to hope for the best.

By noon, Amber had covered a wide area and was tired, hungry, and discouraged. She had taken a few coins with her and used them to buy a sandwich and a raspberry drink. They tasted stale but helped calm her hunger. She sat on a nearby bench to eat and rest, then got up resolutely to continue her combing walk.

The shadows were already long in the street in the late afternoon when she reached one of the last blocks of buildings before the edge of the town. She realized that she had failed and that perhaps she should have asked for help, but from whom? Should she go and speak with the mayor? He had been sympathetic to Kal, and maybe he would help. Yes, that was the best way to go. She had only a few hours before the convoy left, and she had to find Kal before then, or they would miss it.

And suddenly, out of nowhere, there was Kal, right in front of her, smiling and waving to her. "Kal!" she cried, then ran to him, only to find he wasn't there.

An image! He must be nearby. He's projecting an image of himself to let me know he's nearby. That means that he can read my mind! If you can read me, Kal, send me an image that shows where you are.

Right before her eyes appeared the image of Kal, tied to a chair in a dark basement. The image was clear, with a low window at street level. That was her clue! She had to look for a nearby building with a basement window opening onto the street. Amber started to run from building to building, looking for a matching window. Since Kal had been able to read her, he had to be nearby. Only a few buildings were near enough, and five minutes later, she spotted one with a street-level window. She ran to it, her heart beating fast.

"Kal!" she cried.

"I'm here," came Kal's voice through the bars, and Amber felt tears of happiness wetting her cheeks.

"I'm coming to let you out," she reassured him.

"No, wait! The door is locked, and my captor is dangerous— he's the master of ceremonies from the knife-throwing game. He may be back any minute, and he's armed. Where is the gun?"

"It's in the rucksack that I left at the hotel. I took a room when you didn't show up."

"Then go back and fetch it. You'll need it to blow the lock off this door and to defend us if he's back. But please hurry because I don't know what he'll do to me when he returns."

"I'll run as fast as I can, I promise."

Amber turned away from the window and started to run. She forgot that she was tired, that her feet ached, and that it was hours since she last had something to drink. Nothing mattered except getting back on time. She ignored the glances that passersby gave her and kept going even when her lungs ached for oxygen.

***

Amber had run as fast as she could, but getting to the hotel and back had taken almost an hour. It was already dark outside, and she was frantic with worry. If, in the meantime, the evil man had returned, Kal would be in danger. She gave a sigh of relief when she approached the window, whispered Kal's name, and he called out to her.

"You're back. Great! Now you need to find the way to the basement. The entrance may be on the other side."

"I'll find it," Amber said. She took the gun out of the rucksack and circled to the other side of the building. A single door opened in the wall, and through it she saw stairs going up and down. The staircase was in complete darkness, and she groped around the wall for a switch. She found one and switched it on, producing a faint light from a single bulb in the middle of the stairs. It was enough to see where the door was, and she walked down to it.

"Are you here?" she asked, rapping on the door.

"Yes," Kal's muffled voice came through it.

"I'm coming," Amber said.

She rattled the handle, but the door was locked. She took three steps back and pointed the gun at the lock. She didn't know if shooting at it would make a difference. The gun released electromagnetic waves that could be fatal for a human being, but they might not harm a metal lock. Besides, the energy discharged might backfire at her in that small space, and what then? Still, she had to get Kal out of there, and if that meant risking she might get hurt, so be it. She was still debating the best way to use the gun when she heard footsteps approaching. She moved away from the door and into the dark corridor. There she crouched, waiting to see who was coming. A silhouette stopped at the door—in the darkness, she couldn't see his face—and then the sound of a key turning in the lock was followed by the door opening. The man walked in, leaving the door ajar, and Amber tiptoed to it.

"That was a bad wound. I had to rest, but lucky for you, I'm back, or you would be rotting forever in this place. Now, let's talk about my money. Where is it?"

"Turn around and put your hands on your head," came Amber's voice from the door.

The master of ceremonies turned around and gazed at her with contempt.

"And who would you be? Do you think that you can scare me with that toy? Little girls shouldn't be playing with fire," he said, a smirk pasted on his face.

His hand went to his pocket, and Kal cried, "He has a gun!" A second later, a blue light discharged from the gun that Amber held in her hand and hit the master of ceremonies, who fell to the ground. He twitched and kicked for five seconds and then lay still.

"Wait, don't get close before I check him," Kal admonished her. "He's dead," he said after a few seconds. "I can't read his mind. Come here, cut me loose. There is a knife on the floor over there."

Amber stepped over the body of the knife thrower and picked up the knife from the floor.

"Who's that?" she asked, pointing to the body on the floor.

"The knife thrower. It's a long story; I'll tell you later."

Amber cut the ropes that tied Kal to the chair, and he got up, massaging his arms.

"Are you okay?" she asked.

"I'm stiff ... and hurting, but I'll be okay, thanks to you."

"Let's get away, please."

Amber's voice was shaking, and Kal realized that she needed to get away from that grim scene. He limped to the door, helped by Amber, and they climbed the stairs out into the fresh evening air.

CHAPTER 28

At the hotel, they were finally able to speak. They had walked quickly, almost running, without talking much. They glanced back frequently to make sure that nobody was following them. Now in the room, Amber locked the door and threw herself on the bed, breathless.

"That was bad," she said.

She lay with her eyes closed, and Kal, who sat on the bed next to her, tried to understand her feelings without reading her. She had killed a man, and he wasn't sure if she had already processed what she had done. As if reading his thoughts, Amber turned her head away from him, but not quickly enough for him to miss the tear that had started to run down her cheek.

"You saved me," he said softly. "You were very brave."

Amber sat up and wiped the tears from her eyes, this time without trying to hide them.

"I was so scared ... when you didn't come back. I was afraid that I'd never see you again. And I didn't know what to do—"

With the tension behind them, she was at last free to let herself go and let it all out. She was crying now, openly, and Kal knew that he had to do something to comfort her, but what? He had never had to console anybody about anything. In the sterile environment in which he had grown up, people didn't cry, at least not in public. Sorrow was not openly displayed in The City, nor was joy. He allowed himself to follow his instincts and to invite her into his arms. *Funny*, he thought, *how physical contact can be helpful to deal with emotions. And funny how emotions actually play a role in many things. I never knew that.*

They fell into an embrace, and Amber buried her face in his shoulder, letting herself sob until it was over. Five minutes later, the sobs stopped, and she was her composed self again. She straightened up, moved away from the embrace, wiped the last tears from her face, and smiled.

"Thanks for letting me do that. I don't cry a lot, as a rule, but this time I needed it."

"Do you want to talk about it?"

"About what?"

"Your feelings about killing that man. I understand that you are upset and—"

"I'm not upset about that. He was going to hurt you, and I stopped him; that's all there is to it. I would do it again without thinking twice about it."

"Wow! You are tough ... if that's not bothering you, what is?"

"Nothing. It's ... all the tension of the last few days caught up with me, but I'm okay now."

"I'm glad you are. It sort of freaks me out when you lose control."

"I never lose control! To a girl, crying is therapeutic. I can do it or not, as I like. Don't you ever dare think that I'm not in control! Now, please, go and take a shower. You reek like hell. Wear your other clothes. I'll wash these and hope they'll dry out before we have to leave in the morning."

"You think of everything! I'm dying to take a shower, but I also haven't eaten since yesterday. We'll need food. As soon as I'm ready, I'll go out and get some for us to eat here. Safer than going to a restaurant."

"You're not going anywhere without me!" said Amber. "I'm not letting you out of my sight again. I don't want to have to come to your rescue a second time."

"I guess you're right," said Kal. "You have earned your position as my bodyguard, the way you can handle that gun," he joked.

He went into the shower, and she heard the water running. She smiled to herself. She had remembered how vulnerable he looked after falling into the underground river. That led her to imagine how he must look under the shower.

You always pick the wrong time not to read me, you wimp, she thought with a smile.

"I heard that," came the call from the shower.

Amber smiled broadly.

The eatery that the hotel receptionist had directed them to served great meat, fries, and ale. They bought a big dinner that would keep them going for a while and took it to their room. They didn't know when they would eat again and needed the energy. To be on the safe side, they bought extra food to take with them in the morning. As soon as they finished eating, Kal went to lie down on the bed.

"I'm exhausted. I haven't slept since they kidnapped me, if you don't count the time I was out because of the blow to my head. I need to sleep, or I will be useless tomorrow. We have to be at the depot early, so you should do the same."

"I want to take another shower first. All that running has made me sweaty."

"Do that," Kal mumbled, his eyes closed.

When Amber returned from the shower, Kal was already fast asleep in the middle of the bed. She climbed onto the bed and pushed him aside a little to make room for herself. He moved under the pressure of her hands but didn't wake up. She lay beside him and closed her eyes, but a noise from outside the room brought her to her senses. She lay awake, listening to the sounds, but heard nothing more. She had had enough with the hobo who had robbed them and wouldn't let anybody rob them again. She got up, took the gun from the rucksack, and placed it beside the bed for good measure. She was taking her bodyguard duties seriously.

———— · —— · ————

"Wake up! Wake up!"

Amber opened her eyes with an effort, feeling the pressure of Kal's hand on her arm.

"I haven't slept a wink," she complained out of a pasty mouth.

"We overslept. We are going to be late," said Kal.

Amber was immediately fully awake. She sat on the bed and looked around.

"Oh my God!" she said. "We can't miss the convoy."

"We won't, but we need to hurry."

They hastily checked their few belongings. Amber picked up the paper bag with the remains of their evening meal, and Kal shouldered the rucksack. Two minutes later, they went through a silent reception, where they left their key on an empty counter.

"Do you know where to go?" asked Amber.

"More or less. I made inquiries yesterday. It should take us ten minutes to get to the depot."

They almost ran until they reached a fenced compound with a big sign that said "Resurrection Goods Depot." Walking through the gate, they came upon a long line of vehicles. The first one was a truck that looked like a war machine. A grille protected the windshield, and two protruding spear-like beams, one on each side, seemed ready to ram into anything. Lorenson, the convoy leader, stood next to it, yelling at somebody. Seeing them, he stopped screaming and waited for them to approach.

"You're here, good. Go to the second-to-last truck and look for Astrine. You'll be riding with her. Hurry up—we are leaving in five minutes."

Having issued his orders, Lorenson went back to ignoring them. They walked the length of the convoy. Kal counted forty-two vehicles of different sizes and shapes. Some looked new, and others were old and battered. Altogether, they made an odd lot.

A tall, blonde woman of about fifty was checking a tire in the second-to-last truck in line, and they approached her.

"Are you Astrine?"

"Who's asking?" the woman said. Kal and Amber were put off by her unwelcoming posture.

"Lorenson sent us. We are Amber and Kal, and he said that we will ride with you—if you *are* Astrine, that is," Kal said.

"Don't be a smartass," the woman said. "I'm Astrine. Climb into the cab and keep quiet. I need to do some more checks. We are leaving soon, and you're getting in the way."

She turned her back to them and returned to her inspection of the tire. Kal and Amber glanced at each other, then shrugged and climbed into the cab. The truck was small, and the seating space beside the driver wasn't much, but it was a ride, and it would do.

CHAPTER 29

The convoy left the depot, moving like a lazy snake. It negotiated the tortuous road that led from the edge of the town to the top of a high hill and, from there, down into a green valley. A dry creek was the last obstacle before the less-bumpy road that ran through the valley. Once the truck made it without incident, Astrine's expression relaxed, and she even smiled.

"That tire held. I wasn't sure it would. The slope going down that creek is brutal. Changing a tire there is no piece of cake, I can tell you that. So," she said, changing the subject, "you two love-birds are going to be married? Why anybody would want to get married nowadays, the way the world is going, beats me. Look at me—two kids to feed, and this is what I have to do to make ends meet."

"Yes, we are going to get married in Freeland. Amber has family there. We are very grateful to you for taking us. That was very generous," said Kal.

"Generous? Lorenson paid me well. Five silver pieces he paid, and I ain't saying I didn't have to haggle with him over it. Anyway, it's nice to have company on the road. What do you have in that bag that smells so good?"

"Oh, that's the food we took for the road," said Amber. "Would you like some?"

"I can't say I don't," said Astrine.

———— · — · ————

The convoy stopped a half hour before dark, and the trucks formed two concentric circles. Most truck drivers, including Astrine, were old-timers and knew all the ropes. They took their assigned position automatically. Only a few newcomers had to be yelled at by Lorenson before they did it correctly. Then a fire was started at the center of the inner circle, and everybody came to sit beside it. Drinks and food circulated, along with jokes and repartees. The atmosphere was one of camaraderie that Kal had never experienced before.

"So you've done this trip before?" Kal asked Astrine.

"This is my fifth trip—and God permitting, my last one, too. Once I deliver my stuff and get paid for the delivery, I quit. I'll have enough put aside to allow me to take a quiet job, back at home, and still provide for my boys and myself."

"What is it that you are carrying?" Amber asked.

"I don't want to know, and you don't want to, either. There is a reason why they seal those crates. I never ask questions I don't want the answers to. I'm just the delivery girl."

"I'm sorry, I didn't mean to be nosy." Amber was taken aback by Astrine's emphatic answer.

"No harm done," Astrine said, gulping down some more beer.

They sat in silence for a while until Amber grabbed Kal's arm.

"Look there!" she said.

"What?"

"That little boy. What is he doing in a convoy like this?"

"That's Bob's nephew," said Astrine. "The boy is his sister's son. She died last month, and the mayor forced Bob to take care of the boy, so now he's stuck with him. Bob's a bad 'un. The boy would be better off on his own."

Amber got up and approached the boy. A minute later, they came back together.

"Kal, this is Tim," she said.

"How are you, Tim?" Kal asked, giving him a friendly smile to make him feel at ease. "Are you hungry?"

"No, thank you. I've eaten."

"But I bet that the convoy grub doesn't include chocolate," said Kal, pulling out a chocolate bar that he had bought on their last evening in town.

Kal managed to suppress a laugh when Tim snatched the chocolate bar from his hand and devoured it. Amber made him sit on her lap and stroked his hair as he ate.

"How old are you, Tim?" she asked.

"I'll be nine soon," he said.

"Do you like living with your uncle?" Kal asked.

The boy looked around before responding, then spoke in an almost inaudible voice.

"Not much. He beats me," he said.

"Why?" asked Kal.

"I don't know," he answered.

"Told ya he's a bad 'un," said Astrine, shaking her head.

The fire had begun to smolder, and the crowd beside it was dwindling. Tim's uncle beckoned to him, and he ran off. Kal got up, facing Amber and Astrine.

"It has been a long day. We should find a place to sleep," he said.

"You can sleep in the back of the truck," said Astrine. "I take the cab. But whatever you do, make sure that you never go outside the outer circle."

"Why?" asked Kal.

"Because bad people often follow these convoys. Scavengers

who hope to steal something. If you let them, they'll cut your throat to steal your boots. Lorenson's men take turns guarding the circle, but going outside is not safe. If you need to take a piss, go to the outer circle and find a dark space between two trucks. But keep your ears open for suspicious movements. You don't want someone to grab you while you're busy doing that," she added with a bit of a laugh.

"Thanks for warning us," said Kal. "We didn't know that."

"No problem."

Astrine's truck was a closed one like many of the others, and the door wasn't locked. Members of the convoy implicitly trusted one another. Inside, the door kept out the chill of the night, but the room left for them to sleep in wasn't much. Kal dragged a couple of tarpaulins from above a crate and made a makeshift bed with them. They lay there in the almost complete darkness, only broken by a faint light on the wall.

"We'll be there in five days," Amber whispered.

"If all goes well," Kal whispered back.

"It will be all right. We were lucky to find this convoy."

"Yes ..."

"Everything's going to be fine, and we'll make it to Freeland in time to take that stupid chip out of your head."

"I'm tired," said Kal. He turned to one side and closed his eyes. Somehow, he found it hard to share Amber's optimism.

CHAPTER 30

The convoy had traveled uneventfully for the third day and stopped for the night. Everybody was again sitting beside the campfire at the center of the circle. Kal was deep in thought and not paying attention to Amber's chitchat with Astrine. The two women had become friends during the long hours in the cab. They whiled away the time talking about things that Kal barely understood. Girl things. Suddenly, Kal's heart sank, and he jumped to his feet.

"Hey! What's the matter?" Amber asked with surprise.

"I need to talk to you. Not here. Please," he added when Amber grimaced.

She got up, and Kal pulled her by the arm until they reached a quiet corner away from the crowd.

"What's the matter with you?" she complained.

"Someone is planning to attack the convoy," said Kal.

"How do you know that?"

"I was bored with all your girl talk, and I opened my mind a little to kill time."

"And?"

"And I saw it clearly. Someone was thinking of an ambush, someplace near a river and a grove."

"Who?"

"I don't know. I can't say who's thinking what when there are so many people around."

"We must talk to Lorenson."

"But how? How am I going to explain that I know it? I can't tell him that I can read minds. That would put us both in danger. The man is greedy. You saw how he cheated Astrine out of our passage money. If I tell him of my gift, and he realizes that we may be important, there is no telling what he will do."

"You're right. Then tell him that you overheard something," Amber suggested.

"Yes, that's what I'll do. Great idea!"

They returned to the fire, and Lorenson reluctantly agreed to join them for a private conversation.

"So what is it?" he asked once they reached a quiet spot.

"I think that someone is planning to attack the convoy," said Kal.

"Why would you think that?"

"I was going by the trucks in the outer circle, and I heard someone talk about an ambush. He was talking about a grove by a bridge on a river."

"Show him to me."

"I couldn't see him, and I don't know who he is. That's all I heard."

Lorenson was obviously unimpressed.

"Okay. We'll keep our eyes skinned," he said and turned to leave.

"Wait! Are we going to cross a river on a bridge near a grove?"

"Yes, tomorrow. So what?"

"So someone is waiting for us there with an ambush!"

It frustrated Kal to see that Lorenson wasn't taking him seriously.

"Listen, boy. I don't know what you've heard, and I don't care. This is the eleventh time I'm leading a convoy on this road, and I'm pretty sure that if there is any danger, I'll spot it much earlier than you will. We have good scouts and are well armed."

"Can't you take an alternative route? Why take the chance?"

"Any alternative route will cost us a day, so I can't do it. Not on account of things you've heard and probably misunderstood. Have yourself a good night," he concluded and left.

"What are we going to do?" Amber asked anxiously.

"I don't know. We'll think of something. Maybe we should leave the convoy."

"We can't! We would never make it through this country alone. If we had a vehicle, we could try it, but not on foot. We can't waste time and risk being late."

"I try not to think of it, but I know that the clock is ticking for me." Kal turned serious.

"We still have time. We'll find a way," said Amber. She put her hand on his arm and squeezed it in a gesture of encouragement.

"Yes, I'm sure we will," concluded Kal, but he didn't sound too convinced, not even to himself.

"Tim!" Amber exclaimed.

"What about him?"

"We can't let him stay with his uncle. If there is going to be an ambush tomorrow, do you think that he will fight to save the boy?"

"What do you propose?"

"Let's go talk to him."

They went back to the campfire. Tim was sitting with Astrine where they had left him, as he had been doing every evening since the first night.

"Hey, Tim," said Amber, "why don't you travel with us tomorrow? Keep us company."

"Yes!" said Tim enthusiastically.

"Wait a minute," said Astrine. "The cab is crowded as it is. Where do you want me to put him?"

"He can sit on my lap. He needs to spend a few hours away from his uncle, and it will be fun having him with us. He's a sweet boy," Amber said.

"Oh, all right. But talk to Bob," said Astrine grudgingly.

Amber nodded and strode to where Tim's uncle was standing, talking and drinking with a couple of other men.

"Yes?" he inquired as she approached.

"We wanted your permission to take Tim on our truck for the day tomorrow. We'd love to have him keep us company during the day."

"You can have 'im any time. He's a pain in the ass, that boy."

"Thank you," said Amber, but Tim's uncle had gone back to drinking with his friends and ignoring her.

Kal and Amber had debated whether to tell Astrine of the ambush. After discussing it, they decided against it. She surely would not believe them, just like Lorenson didn't, so there was no point. Throughout the next day, they traveled in tense silence. They scanned the surrounding landscape for signs of an ambush, and after a while, Astrine gave up trying to make conversation. It was early afternoon when they reached the top of a high hill, and Kal sat up, suddenly alert. Tim had fallen asleep, his head on Amber's lap and his feet all the way across Kal and out the window. In the distance, a grove dotted the slopes leading to the entrance to a canyon. To reach the grove, the road descended the hill and crossed a bridge.

"Stop, please. Stop the truck!" Kal said.

"What? Why?" cried Astrine.

"There is going to be an ambush after that bridge. We are in danger. Please stop!"

Astrine applied the brakes, and the truck stopped abruptly. The truck after them, the last one of the convoy, overtook them, and the driver opened the window.

"Problems?" he asked.

"Oil pressure," Astrine answered. "Go ahead. We'll catch up with you."

The other truck went on, and Astrine turned to Kal.

"What is this nonsense about an ambush? How would you know about that?"

"I overheard—"

"And didn't think to tell Lorenson?"

"I did, but he didn't take me seriously."

Astrine gazed at Kal with contempt.

"Lorenson is a pro. If he isn't taking you seriously, it's because there is nothing worth paying attention to."

She threw the truck into gear, and it started moving again.

"I'll yet be sorry that I've taken these kids with me!" Kal cried.

"What?" Astrine said. She applied the brakes again and gaped at Kal.

"That's what you were thinking, weren't you?" said Kal.

"You can read minds?"

"Yes. That's how I learned about the ambush. And I saw an image of the place, which was exactly what we see down there. We can't go there."

"What am I thinking now?" Astrine asked.

"This boy may be crazy, but I have two kids to look after and can't risk ending up dead," said Kal.

"That's it. I'm convinced. You're a freak, but I'm convinced. What do we do now?"

"Let's back up, so we're hidden behind the hill, and see what happens. If I'm wrong and nothing happens, we'll catch up with them. And if not ...."

Kal didn't have to finish his sentence. They all knew what the alternative meant. Astrine put the truck in reverse, and soon it was hidden behind the hill. Tim had woken up, and his "What's happening?" questions went unanswered. The four of them got out and went to the top to look down. The first truck had reached the bridge and would soon enter the canyon. They waited patiently as the snake-like convoy passed over the bridge. When the last truck was about to enter the canyon, numerous figures appeared behind the grove's trees. A loud explosion came from afar, smoke rose above the canyon, and then the noise of antiquated firearms reached their ears.

"My God!" Astrine exclaimed, and that kind of summed it up.

CHAPTER 31

As soon as the noise of the ambush had made itself heard from down below, Astrine had turned the truck around and pushed on the accelerator. Amber had explained gently to Tim what was happening, and he had remained silent for a while.

"Is Uncle dead?" he had finally asked.

"We hope he's okay," Amber had said.

"I hope he's dead," Tim said and clammed up.

They drove in silence, each with their own thoughts. When they reached a junction, almost one hour later, Astrine stopped the truck.

"Here is where we should take the alternative route to Freeland," Astrine said.

"Are you sure?" Amber asked.

Without responding, Astrine pulled a greasy old map from her glove compartment and spread it over Amber's thighs.

"Look here," she said, pointing to the map. "This is where the ambush happened, and this is where we are now. If we turn right here and follow this road, we'll get to a different bridge. That's downstream from the planned crossing point. Then we'll have to turn up north to get back on the main road to Freeland."

Kal, who sat next to the door, had to crane his neck to follow the explanations on the map. He nodded in assent.

"Yes, that looks right," he agreed, "but we need to find a place to spend the night. I don't think it would be wise to do the crossing in the dark."

"If they are not coming after us," Amber pointed out.

"They have a rich convoy to feast on," said Astrine gloomily. "I don't think they'll waste energy coming after one lousy truck—if they notice that we are missing at all."

"I agree. Pilaging the convoy must keep them busy for quite some time. What is this place here? It's a small detour from our way," said Kal, pointing to a place on the map.

"It's an old, abandoned abbey. I've been there once, many years ago."

"It's high on a cliff and has a back exit road. If we can get there before dark, it could be a good place to spend the night. We could make sure that nobody's coming after us."

"We need to be careful with the gas, or we may get stuck. Taking the longer road is going to cost us, and I don't want to waste any more gas than we have to. Anyway, let's decide when we get there."

By the time they got to the road leading to the abbey, it was almost dark. Astrine turned onto the side road without saying anything. It was a short road, but steep and dangerously winding, and Kal felt better when the truck drove through the gate of what once was a large complex. Now, only the ruins of what had been the central building remained standing. The rest was rubble. Astrine stopped the truck behind the remains of a high stone wall, where it couldn't be seen from the road below.

"The epicenter of The Pulse wasn't far from here," said Astrine, but nobody felt like commenting.

"We don't have any food," said Amber, speaking somberly.

"It's all gone with the supply truck, but we have plenty of water in the back, and that's more important," said Astrine.

"That can't be helped. We should sleep and leave at dawn, but we need to keep guard. We don't want any surprises. I'll do the first shift, and I'll wake you up when I'm too tired to go on," said Kal, speaking to Amber.

"I can do my part, too," Astrine said.

"You need to drive, and that's work enough. I can sleep on the road."

Astrine nodded, started to climb into the cab, then stopped and stepped down again, a blanket in her hand.

"Take it," she said to Kal, who took it. "Come up with me," she then said to Tim.

"Okay," said Tim, and went after her.

Kal said good night to Amber in the back of the truck and went to sit on a low stone wall facing the road below. The night was chilly, and he covered his shoulders with the blanket. The moon was almost full and shone on the valley, allowing Kal to see both the road to the abbey and the main road below clearly. *There will be no surprises here*, he thought. He repressed the temptation to listen in on what Amber and Astrine were thinking. Instead, to kill time, he counted the rocks that dotted the hillside. A few had odd shapes, and he assigned each of them a character—one was a sheep, another a ball, and so on.

A touch on his shoulder made him jerk around.

"You scared me!" he exclaimed. "What are you doing out here?"

"I couldn't sleep," said Amber. "And while you keep guard, shouldn't you do it with your mind, too? You would have known that I was sneaking up on you. It's cold here," she commented, sitting beside him. She opened his blanket and sat closer so Kal could cover her with it. "Better this way," she said. "So, what am I thinking?"

"You know I don't eavesdrop on you."

"It's not eavesdropping if you have permission. Go ahead and do it."

"I don't understand. You're here and can speak for yourself, so why should I read your mind?"

"Because, you ox, some things are difficult to explain with words ... or to say."

"Okay ..."

Kal closed his eyes and opened his mind. It took him a second to read Amber's thoughts, but he remained still, eyes closed, for a full minute, absorbing their meaning. Then he opened his eyes and gazed at her, unsure what Amber expected of him.

"So you ... since when?"

"It's been a while now. I realized it when you were on that platform, facing the knife." She lowered her eyes, kept silent for a moment, and then continued. "I wanted you to know because who knows what will happen to us tomorrow. Or the day after. But it's okay; you don't have to feel the same way."

Kal kept his eyes on her, struggling with the words.

"But I do," he said at last.

"You do?" Amber said, lifting her gaze to look into his eyes. "You aren't just being nice to me?"

"No. I don't think so. I mean, I've never felt this way before, and I'm confused. We never talked about these things in The City. To us, love was something archaic, some ancient custom that interfered with progress. We chose our mates on a scientific basis. The aim was to improve the health and quality of the population, not to satisfy some stupid whim. But now I understand that the so-called 'whim' is a wonderful thing. Does any of this make sense to you?"

"More than you think."

"So now what?"

"Close your eyes."

Kal complied, and Amber got up, gently wriggling out of the blanket. She faced him and then sat on his thighs. She took his face in her hands, and her lips gently met his. Slowly, sweetly, she kissed him, and he responded with the same gentleness. When she finally moved her face away from him, Kal opened his eyes.

"I'm dizzy," he said with a vapid smile.

Amber laughed and caressed his cheek.

"More," said Kal, closing his eyes again.

Amber kissed him again, this time deeper. His hands went up to her back, pulling her closer, but she moved away and got up.

"There will be a time for us to explore these feelings better, but now is not the right time. Not here, not now," she said.

"You're right, damn it! But you shouldn't tease me like that," said Kal.

"I shouldn't, I know. I didn't mean to tease. I'll go now."

"Wait!"

"What?"

"Say it," said Kal. "I want to hear it."

"I said it in my mind. You heard."

"Sometimes, my mind plays tricks on me. I want to hear it with my own ears, from your lips."

"Good night, Kal," said Amber with a broad smile. She kissed him lightly for the last time and was gone.

CHAPTER 32

The following day, at dawn, Kal knocked on the cab's door. He had kept guard all night, dozing off for a few minutes now and then when he felt safe enough that nobody was coming after them. Anyway, in the stillness of the deserted area, anybody approaching would make enough noise to alert him. Astrine was asleep with Tim hugging her under the blanket.

"He reminds me of my boys," she said almost apologetically when Kal smiled at the scene.

As soon as everybody was up and organized, they left the abbey and reached the bridge across the river. Five hours later, they rejoined the main road, ending their detour. The route took them through an endless, uninhabited plain. They drove on, and by afternoon, they reached a settlement. All there was to it was a large yard, a main building, and a handful of small houses dotted around.

"This is August's Place," said Astrine. "We stop here. It's the last trading place before Freeland, where we can get food and gas. I don't have much money, but it should be enough for the gas."

"We'll pay for everything, Astrine," said Kal. "We owe you."

"I won't argue with you," she said.

They stepped off the truck. The door of the main building opened, and a middle-aged woman came out.

"August!" Astrine cried.

"Is that you, Astrine? Come here, you old witch!" she shouted back.

The two women hugged and kissed on the cheeks.

"I thought that I had seen the last of you, or so you said last year," said August.

"I was planning to, but I needed some more money, so I decided to make a last trip."

"But how come you're here all alone? Where is the convoy?"

"There was an ambush. There is no convoy. We are the only ones who got away."

"Ambushed? That is awful! You need to tell me everything."

"I will, but August, dear, we haven't eaten in two days."

"How stupid of me! Of course, you must be starving. Come on in. I'll get you something immediately. Anything else you need right now?"

"A shower," Amber hazarded.

"First we eat," Astrine said decisively.

——— · — · ———

After a satisfying meal, August assigned them rooms in two small, one-room houses. They didn't have to discuss sleeping arrangements. Tim went with Astrine without asking questions. The shower was in a small structure outside, with water heated by a kerosene stove. The door had no lock, so Kal kept guard while Amber showered. He accompanied her back to their room and then went to shower too. Coming back, he knocked on Astrine's door in the building next to theirs, but there was no response. He opened the door and saw that Tim was in bed, asleep, alone. He slept peacefully, and Kal withdrew quietly to avoid waking him up. Astrine had to be still chatting with August. After dinner, August had monopolized her, demanding updates and gossip, and they hadn't had a chance to plan for the next day.

Entering their room, Kal saw Amber still drying her hair with a towel. She was dressed in a bathrobe with an "August's Place" symbol, a rooster crowing at a star.

"I'm spoiled," she said, smiling brightly. "This is a great place."

"It sure is." Kal paused for a moment, then continued, "We are going to sleep in this bed, right?"

"Sleeping is all we are going to do, you know that. For now."

"Yes, but—"

Kal was going to argue the wisdom of putting good things off for an uncertain tomorrow, but he didn't get a chance. Astrine barged unannounced into the room.

"Get dressed. Quickly!" she ordered.

"What's the matter? Why now?"

"Because—and keep your voices down—it turns out that you are precious. Word was sent to all settlements, stations, and towns between Freeland and The City that you must be captured. Whoever captures you will be rewarded. There is a bounty on your heads, one that would keep me in luxury for years to come. August is going to share it with me—except that there will be no prize. We're going to get out of here before she can organize a capture party. So now step on it!"

"Oh, my God!" Amber exclaimed.

"We can explain," Kal said.

"'My God' is right, and explanations can wait. I have told August that I'm going to fill up my tank now so I'm ready to leave first thing in the morning. The gas station is outside, and as soon as we have filled up, I'll step on the gas, and we'll get the hell away from here. I told her that you are armed to the teeth and dangerous and that she should wait for you to fall asleep in this room before she attempts to capture you. You'll need to sneak out and get in the back of the truck where nobody can see you. At the gas station, you can get out and join me in the cab. Clear?"

"Yes. We don't know how to thank you," said Kal. He found it difficult to keep emotions out of his voice.

"Yeah, yeah. Save it for later. I need to pick Tim up, and then I'll wait for you in the cab. Once you are inside, knock three times to let me know."

Kal nodded, and she left.

"Turn around," Amber ordered. "Now you can turn back," she said after a few moments. "I'm dressed."

They left the room, closing the door silently behind them. Kal kept his rucksack on his left shoulder, his right hand inside, holding the gun at the ready. They ran, keeping to the shadows cast by the buildings, and tiptoed around the main building until they reached the truck. Kal opened the door, and they jumped inside. They closed it carefully to avoid making noise. Amber knocked three times on the wall. The engine started, and the truck moved immediately. A minute later, it stopped, and Kal and Amber jumped down.

"Quick! Bring the pump," Astrine ordered while she opened the fuel cap.

The pump was old and asthmatic, and refueling was nerve-racking, but eventually, the tank was full. They jumped in, Amber held a sleepy Tim on her lap, and Astrine released the brake.

"I've paid her in advance for the fuel, so she can't say that I stole from her," Astrine said while she started the engine. "But I guess this is going to be my last trip anyway. I won't be a welcome guest here anymore."

"Astrine, you're—" Amber started to say.

"Save it!" Astrine interrupted her. "I know, I'm a stupid senti-mentalist. I wasted my chance for a large reward for capturing two dangerous fugitives. That's who I am. Only you don't look dangerous to me, and whatever trouble you're in, I don't want to know. I'm no turncoat, and nobody—nobody—will ever be able to say that I betrayed my fellow travelers. Those who broke their bread with me and with whom I shared dangers and hardship are sacred to me. That's the code that I live by. Period!"

"That's very noble, Astrine," said Kal.

"Shut up! Don't make me regret it," she said with a sigh.

The truck traveled at high speed on the good, straight road, and in a few minutes, the lights of August's Place disappeared behind them. Kal allowed himself to slump down in his seat and close his eyes. Amber's hand found his and squeezed it, and he finally fell asleep, his head on Amber's shoulder.

CHAPTER 33

"Wake up, Kal, we've arrived!"

Amber's voice brought Kal back from the deep sleep into which he had finally slipped, the first after a long string of fitful and fragmented nights. In the distance, wide gates opened into high walls that extended on both sides as far as the eye could see.

"Is that ..."

"The trading post, yes," Astrine said. "Read the sign."

High above the gates, the sign said "Freeland Trading Post." As the truck reached it, three armed guards came out of a side door and signaled for them to stop.

"Bill of goods," one said curtly.

"Here you go," said Astrine, handing him a sheaf of papers.

"Here it says that you are with Lorenson's Convoy Eleven. There should be forty-two trucks. Where are the rest?"

"We are all that remains of the convoy. There was an ambush. The others ... may God have mercy on their souls."

"That's bad news. I'll have to report it. Anyway, your papers are in order, and you can come in."

The guard signaled to the gates, and they opened to reveal a large yard. A long building, equipped with goods-discharge bays of varying heights and lengths, marked its edge.

"Go to bay seven," said the guard, and Astrine drove forward and then turned to back into the bay.

A man in uniform came from inside and walked up to them. He gave instructions for unloading the truck and then handed Astrine a document.

"These two are on the bill signed by Lorenson, but who's this boy here?" he asked, looking at Tim.

"He's my son," Astrine said. "Write that down."

"Umpf! Why isn't he on the bill?"

"I don't know. Lousy paperwork. Who cares?"

The man hesitated for a moment, then took the document back from Astrine. He wrote something on it and gave it back to her.

"This will get you all lodging during the quarantine period," he said.

"Quarantine?" Amber said. "What quarantine?"

"There is a new quarantine policy. The last convoy brought infectious diseases, so now everybody has to stay in quarantine for five days. You need to refer to medical inspection after that period for an entrance permit into Freeland."

"But we can't!" Kal said. "We can't stay here. If we have to wait five days, it will be too late."

"Boy," said the man, "I don't know what you're talking about, but that's your problem, not mine. I need to warn you that people trying to avoid quarantine are shot on sight, so you'd better keep your patience and wait it out."

With those words, he turned and left.

"What are we going to do? I'm running out of time with my chip," Kal said in despair.

"I know. We'll think of something," Amber encouraged him.

"Isn't your uncle the ruler of Freeland or something? Why didn't you tell that man?"

"He's the chairman of the Council of Freeland. We need to get in touch with him, but arguing with these people is no good."

"Why?"

"Because this is an autonomous zone. These are outside contractors, not Freeland people. They contract with Freeland but are not under its rule."

"That's bad," said Kal.

"I've no idea what you're talking about," said Astrine, "but save it for later. We need to go and find lodging before a new convoy comes in and snatches all the good places."

"You go ahead and get rooms for the four of us. We'll catch up with you," said Amber.

"All right. There is a tavern in the central square. That's where I'll be after I book the rooms. Take your arrival papers. You'll need them to get around here." Astrine handed the papers to Amber and started to leave, but Amber's voice stopped her.

"Wait!" she said. She went over and hugged Astrine, who hugged her back after a brief moment of consternation.

"What was that for?" she asked.

"If anything should happen to us and we don't meet again. I want to thank you for being a wonderful friend and a great person," said Amber, speaking somberly.

"Take this," said Kal. He walked up to Astrine and handed her his purse, which she took after a brief hesitation.

"What is this?" she asked. "Is it all your money? It's a lot; I can't take it. And you will need money, too."

"It's okay," said Kal. "Let's say that you are guarding our money for us. But if we don't meet again, it will be more useful to you than to us. We won't need it where we are going."

Astrine nodded. She understood.

"Tim ..." said Amber, opening her arms, and Tim ran into her embrace.

"You're leaving us, right? I won't see you again," said Tim with the perceptiveness that children sometimes have.

"I don't know, Tim. I truly don't, but if we don't meet here again, I'm sure that Astrine will take good care of you."

"I will, you know that," said Astrine. "I don't know what you're up to, but you worry me. Don't do anything stupid. You've heard that man. They shoot you on sight."

"We'll be careful," said Amber, "and if we don't see each other again here, one day we'll look you up in Resurrection."

"Damn stupid dust," said Astrine, wiping an ill-concealed tear. "Go now!"

Amber and Kal nodded and walked away rapidly.

"Do you know where to go?" asked Kal.

"Not exactly, but the Freeland Council must have an office somewhere here, and we need to find it. This isn't a big place; let's look around."

They had to ask a few times before someone directed them to a narrow street, where he said they would find many commercial offices. They finally reached a door with a sign that said "Freeland Council Representative." They walked in and up a flight of stairs until they reached an ornate door. They pushed it and found themselves in a dark, cool room. Opening the door had shaken a bell, producing steps and, a few seconds later, a pot-bellied man.

"Hello," said the man cheerfully. "My name is Julian. What can I do for you?"

"We urgently need your help," said Amber. "I am Chairman Afex's niece."

The man looked incredulous and eyed them with suspicion.

"That's an extraordinary claim. You see, we know that the chairman's niece is elsewhere—I can't divulge more details, of course," said the man, acting important.

"You don't need to. I was in The City, and now I'm here. I need your immediate help; failing which, Freeland will suffer irreparable harm. Do you get that?"

"How do you propose that I ascertain your identity?"

"Let me speak with my uncle."

"My, my—that's not so easy. We're not in Freeland here, properly speaking, and facilities are not advanced. I may have a communication line; let's see," he said, looking at an old clock that hung from a wall, "in about one hour. Until then, why don't we sit down and you tell me what you need? That way, we can be, ahem, more productive when we speak with the chairman?"

"Sure. We need to leave here without delay. Today."

"May I see your arrival papers?" he asked, and Amber gave them to him.

"So that's the issue. You want to jump quarantine. It can't be done. The penalty is death."

"We have to."

"But why all this impatience? Wait for five days, and you're free to leave. This is not a bad place to wait in. A little boring, perhaps, but comfortable."

"I can't explain, but we can't stay here."

"Well, let's wait for the communication line. Perhaps the chairman can talk some sense into you."

They waited in silence. Julian brought tea and cookies, and they acknowledged them with a grateful nod but only stared at them. When the time for the call finally came, Julian spoke into a strange, horn-shaped communicator and then nodded and handed it to Amber.

"Amber, is it you? Are you okay?" came Afex's anxious voice over the line.

"It's me, Uncle. I'm fine."

"I'm so relieved. We heard so many things, so much misinformation ... I didn't know what to think. Thank God we'll be seeing you soon."

"Uncle, listen—we can't wait out the quarantine. We need to get to you now. In a few hours at most. I can't explain right now, but we're running out of time. It's a matter of life or death."

"You are asking me to disobey our own laws. Putting the quarantine in place was our Council's demand after we got hit by a contagious disease. I have no authority. I would have to ask for the Council's permission."

"No time for that. If you don't come to get us now, it will be too late."

A long silence ensued.

"Give me Julian again," Afex said at last.

Julian held the receiver to his ear, saying "yes" from time to time, and then he replaced it in its cradle.

"In two hours, you'll be out of here," he said.

Amber smiled. "Now we can have tea," she said.

CHAPTER 34

"Time to go," Julian said.

"Where?" Amber asked.

"To the roof. Follow me."

They left through the ornate door and climbed three flights of stairs, stopping before a closed metal door.

"We wait here until we get the signal," Julian said.

They stood in silence in the dark, and Kal took Amber's hand and locked fingers with her.

"You are amazing, you know?" Kal whispered in her ear.

"Say it again when we're safe," she whispered back.

"I say it now, and I'll say it again. Always."

"Cut it out!" Amber said, with a laugh, when Kal's lips touched her cheek in the dark. "Not a good time for that."

"Only whispering," said Kal, jokingly, "to ease the tension of waiting."

"Here they are. Come after me," Julian said. He pushed the door open, and a whiff of cold air hit their faces.

A strong vibration came from above. They forced their eyes to focus, and a dark disk was clearly outlined against the sky above their heads. A lighted staircase appeared almost by magic, and Julian urged them to go forward.

"Go on, climb in. Quickly!" he ordered.

Kal pushed Amber up the first step and then jumped on it himself. They climbed up and into an empty compartment within the aircraft. As soon as they both completed the climb, the staircase folded up, and the compartment door closed.

"Sit down!" a voice boomed over a loudspeaker. Then, without warning, the aircraft jumped sideways, sending them both rolling on the floor.

The aircraft eventually stabilized and changed pace into a smooth flight. The compartment they had entered had a door facing inward. It opened, and a middle-aged, stout man stood in the doorframe.

"Uncle!" Amber cried. She ran to him and hugged him.

"My God, Amber," he said, smiling broadly, "you look like a hobo. Where have you been?"

"I've been around enough. I'm dying to tell you all about it, but first, let me introduce you to Kal."

"Oh, yes, we've heard about you," said Afex, extending a hand for Kal to shake. "We have sources in The City, and we heard rumors."

"Sir," said Kal, speaking emotionally, "first of all, I want to thank you for coming for us so qui—." Kal didn't finish the sentence. He stared at Afex, and then his eyes rolled back, and he dropped to the ground. A few seconds later, his arms and legs started jerking uncontrollably. It was apparent that he had difficulty breathing. Afex knelt beside him and looked up at Amber.

"He's having an epileptic seizure," he said. "Let's hope it's not a long one."

"No, Uncle!" Amber cried. "It's his chip. It's in self-destruct mode. Oh my God—we must get him to a surgeon. We must get it out of his head!"

"Wait by him," Afex ordered. He ran from the compartment

and immediately returned. "Sit down. The aircraft is going to accelerate too much to stand. We are taking him to the Salamex medical center. The captain is talking to the medical crew there, and they'll be ready for him."

Amber was on the floor beside Kal, who had stopped twitching and was hardly breathing. She held his hand, crying.

"We thought that he had two more days. Two more days, that's all we needed ... what will I do if ... if ...."

"We'll make it in time. I promise," said Afex, but his voice didn't carry conviction.

An emergency crew was waiting for Kal at the medical center and rushed him into the operating room. There was nothing more that Amber could do except wait outside. She paced the small waiting room restlessly while Afex watched her, helpless. After a while, he walked up to her and held her in his arms.

"He's in good hands; don't torment yourself. Doctor Armond is a wonderful neurosurgeon. He couldn't do any better. I gather he's special to you," he said after a brief pause, speaking soothingly.

"He is. Very special. Not only to me but also to Freeland and to everybody else. Let me tell you who Kal is."

"My informants tell me that he worked at the physics laboratories and that he's a brilliant young physicist."

"All that, and also he's the one who discovered how to neutralize the virtual reality component of the chip. That's the component that makes people believe that the world is different from what it is; the one that Father rebelled against, which allows Alvin to keep the people imprisoned in a fool's paradise. That's how important Kal is. He's so important that I gave up trying to rescue Father to get him here."

"And he hasn't shared his discovery with you or with anybody else?"

"I don't have the background needed to understand it. He had to flee The City on the day he made his discovery, so no—if he dies, his secret dies with him. And I ... I ...."

Amber broke down in tears, and all Afex could do was to let her bury her face in the hollow of his shoulder. He kept holding her until the waiting room door opened, and a man in a white robe came in. Amber turned to face him, and his serious expression made her heart stop.

"Doctor Armond. Is he—?"

"We managed to remove the chip with minimal damage to his brain matter. But the chip was melting before we got to it, and did some damage before we removed it."

"And?"

"And we don't know how serious the damage is. We won't know until he stabilizes. We need to be optimistic and hope for the best. We will transfer him to a room in half an hour, and you'll be able to see him then."

"Thank you," said Amber, sniffing and wiping the tears from her eyes.

The doctor turned to leave but stopped at the door.

"Amber," he said.

"Yes?"

"Please, don't get your hopes up too much," he said without looking at her, and then he left.

CHAPTER 35

For five days, Kal had lain in bed without regaining consciousness. And for five days, Amber had sat beside him, hardly leaving his room in the hope of seeing a sign indicating that he might wake up. Doctor Armond had visited often, and other doctors had come and gone. At first, doctor visits were more frequent, but after his vital signs stabilized, a doctor came to check on him only occasionally. Afex had come often to support her, but his visits had become shorter and shorter.

"I'd like to stay longer and keep you company," he had said, "but I'm afraid that recent events require my presence at headquarters."

"Why? What's happening?"

"I don't want to worry you. You have enough things on your mind as it is."

"I'm a big girl, and I can handle anything. Tell me."

"There have been rumors circulating, as well as other signs, and we fear that an attack by The City is not too far off. You know about New City, of course."

"The colony they established near our northern borders? Of course, but it's a small place. It can't be a threat to us. I never understood why they put it there, where there is only desert and no natural resources."

"I often wondered about that, too, but now it's clear. Our spies tell us that the area of New City is now five times the original. It has been populated with people from The City to full capacity. Of course, they don't know that they are living in a desert and eating out of The City's hands. They think that they are meant to live in paradise—the augmented reality broadcast to them is stunning."

"So what's the problem with them? Let them live in their fool's paradise."

"The problem is that they are the outpost for an attack on us by The City. They are manipulated into believing that we are poisoning their land. The City is arming and training them for the day when we will destroy their paradise."

"But we are not going to, right? So how are those fibs going to help The City?"

"Don't you see? They will tune the augmented reality to show that their paradise is gradually dying out. Then, the City-appointed rulers of New City will convince them that they need the help of The City to stop us. The City will send its forces to 'protect' New City, and the attack on Freeland will begin."

"But why such a complicated plot? Why not use The City's power to attack us? They don't need an excuse, so why isn't that simpler?"

"To be successful, an attack on Freeland needs a base, soldiers, supplies, and equipment. They need to harass us, wear out our resources, and keep us in a constant state of alarm, which we can't maintain forever. New City will provide all that. The Immaculates make up a relatively small force, but they are well-trained and can lead the mass of field soldiers trained in New City. New City is nothing short of a military base. The motivation they are building is their hatred toward us. They think that they are pioneers building a new tomorrow in dreamland, and that we are working to rob them of their dream and destroy their lives. Do you see now? New City is not a real settlement—it is an army camp. Ironically, the people who live there don't know that they are soldiers—yet. They would never dream that The City may sacrifice them for its goals."

"That's awful! What demonic ideas!"

"Demonic is right."

"So, what are we doing?"

"We are getting ready. All citizens seventeen years old or older are getting military training. You would be called to do it, too, under different circumstances."

"But that's hardly a real army. If New City is so heavily armed and dangerous, how is this going to help us?"

"Frankly, I don't know. We never needed a massive army—our regular military numbers less than a thousand. Our recruits will have to bear the burden of defending us. We have no choice."

"Unless there is another way," said Amber, gazing at Kal.

"We can't count on that. When the time comes, we will be as ready as we can."

After that conversation, Afex left feeling a little better. He hated keeping things from Amber, no matter how unpleasant they were. Amber went back to watching Kal, relegating thoughts of New City and fears of war to the back of her mind. From time to time, she approached the bed and held his hand, but it always remained limp. Sitting with him was tiring. The stress of waiting for a sign of awakening that didn't come wore her out, and soon she fell asleep in her armchair.

A sound jerked her awake. A moan. She jumped to her feet and ran to the bed. Kal had opened his eyes and was looking around with a disoriented expression.

"Where am I?" he asked feebly.

"Kal, oh, thank God!"

Amber took his hand, and tears of happiness ran down her cheek. Kal gazed at her intently and in silence for a few seconds.

"Who are you?" he asked at last.

The movement in Kal's bed had triggered an alarm. That had sent a doctor and a nurse running into the room to find Amber gaping at Kal, aghast. They started getting busy around Kal, checking him, taking measurements, and asking questions. When they finished, the doctor spoke to Amber.

"Well, this is a surprise. We didn't think that he would wake up."

"Doctor," Amber said, whispering so Kal wouldn't hear, "he didn't recognize me. How can that be?"

The doctor nodded and placed his arm around her shoulder, leading her out of the room.

"The damage to his brain was not insignificant. Loss of memory is by no means unexpected. But it doesn't have to be permanent," he said.

"What can I do?"

"Be patient. Talk to him and remind him. Help him remember. But please, don't wear him out. He needs to rest. Ten minutes at most today, agreed?"

Amber nodded in assent and walked pensively back into the room.

"Kal, don't you remember me?" she asked.

"Should I? What's your name?"

"Yes, you should, and you will ... eventually. I'm sure of that. I'm Amber. We've been through a lot together. Try to remember."

"Amber ... I'm sorry, but it doesn't ring a bell."

She sat on his bed, close to him. Kal peered into her face with a puzzled look but gave no sign of recognition.

"The last thing that I remember was going to a bar with my friend, Janec. I must've drunk something wrong and fainted. And these bandages," he added, touching his head for the first time. "I guess I've fallen and hurt my head. Which hospital is this, City Central?

"No, it's not," said the doctor, who had walked into the room. He injected a drug into Kal's vein. "Now you need to rest. Here, this will put you to sleep. You can ask all the questions in the morning."

———— · —— · ————

"I thought that it was a dream, a nightmare," said Kal. He sat, pensive, in the armchair in which the doctor had allowed him to move the following day. "I remember the pastures and birds disappearing and the landscape changing before my eyes. I thought it was a dream inspired by my experience in my lab. And you say that it was true?"

"It was," said Amber.

"And you were there with me?"

"I was."

"I think I remember you. I have a faint image of you in my mind. What else happened after that?"

Amber embarked on the long, complex task of telling Kal all they had gone through together. He listened, often with disbelief on his face, asking a few questions. He was a good listener.

"Are you sure that I did all those things? It doesn't sound quite like me."

"It's not at all like you ... as you were at first. You changed a lot during this journey—and I liked the new you better," she added with a smile.

"Then I'll have to change again." Kal smiled back. "Will you help me?"

"I'll do what I can."

The door opened to let Afex in.

"I heard the good news," he said, smiling broadly.

"Kal, this is my uncle, Afex. I told you about him," said Amber.

Afex grabbed Kal's hand and shook it warmly.

"You saved my life," said Kal, without letting go of Afex's hand.

"Well, actually, it was Amber. When she gets something into her head, there is no stopping her. This time it was getting you here in time, never mind that she could have been shot for it." Afex smiled at Amber with affection.

"Thank you," said Kal, looking at Amber with a serious face. "You didn't tell me that."

Amber made a noncommittal gesture and looked away.

"I'm so glad to meet you, Kal," said Afex. "I want to thank you for taking care of Amber. She told me everything you did for her, and I admire the way you looked after each other. I'm happy that you are back. The doctor tells me you'll be better soon and that he'll allow you to walk around. Unfortunately," he went on, switching to a somber expression, "we can't let you rest too much. The situation may force our hand soon, and we need your help now, I'm afraid. As soon as the doctor allows us, we will need you to get to work."

"Why the rush?" asked Amber.

"Things are moving faster than we thought. Our informants tell us that The City's plans have been accelerated."

"Sorry, but I'm not following you at all," said Kal. "What is the problem, and what do you expect me to help with?"

"Let me grab a chair, and I'll tell you all about it. It's a lot of information to digest," said Afex with a sigh.

——— · — · ———

Kal made good progress, at least as far as his physical condition was concerned. But his memory wasn't coming back. And the worst part was that the many years of City indoctrination had not disappeared, and his City manners had resurfaced. His inhibitions and the quirks were all back. It was hard on Amber, who spent hours in his room trying to reconnect with him.

"I wish you could still read my mind," said Amber one day when she felt too exasperated by the distance he was keeping from her. "That was the one good thing that came with your damned chip."

"You told me about it, but frankly, I can't remember reading minds. I don't know how that could happen."

"Kal, look at me!" she ordered. "Do you remember kissing me?"

"No, please! Don't talk like that," said Kal, blushing.

"Let me remind you." Amber drew close, slowly so as not to scare him, but her eyes met those of a terrified Kal.

"I'm sorry," he said, turning away from her. "It doesn't feel right."

"I need you to remember, and you're not helping!"

"Perhaps I'll never remember. Nothing of what you said feels real to me, and frankly, much of it is embarrassing. Hearing things that you say I did makes me uncomfortable. Those memories may be gone forever."

"Don't say that! They can't be gone. The doctor said that in time you will remember."

"Yes ... but in the meantime ... I'm sorry if I'm not who you want me to be. Maybe you should stay away from me until I remember ... if I remember."

"Do you *want* me to stay away?"

Kal fixed his gaze on the floor without responding, and Amber got up and left, hanging her head.

CHAPTER 36

Amber resolved to keep her distance from Kal until his memory returned—if it did. But despite her resolve, she had let her uncle talk her into continuing to see Kal.

"He needs you," Afex had said. "He asks about you all the time."

"But when I'm with him, he is somebody else and keeps pushing me away. It's too hard for me to see him like that, behaving like a perfect stranger."

"He has sparks of memory, but the doctors say that he isn't able to hold on to them. They think that your presence would have a stabilizing influence on him. We can't afford to lose his cooperation now; you know that."

"All right, Uncle. I'll spend time with him if you think it will help."

Afex had set up a laboratory for Kal, with all the equipment that he had asked for. He had issued orders that Kal was to have access to anything he wanted. Kal had wanted a bed in the lab because sometimes he needed to sleep by his equipment to check on an experiment. For the past two weeks, since leaving the hospital, he had practically lived in the lab. He ate and slept there—that is, he ate when he remembered to eat and slept when he fell off his feet at the end of a twenty-hour workday. He had kept requesting more equipment to the point that his laboratory looked like a junkyard. On her first visit, Amber had convinced him to leave the building and sit in the sun for a few minutes, but he had soon asked to go back inside.

"This place makes me nervous," he had said. "All these insects and birds flying around. Not to speak of the dogs and cats ... I had only seen them in documentaries before."

"But don't you feel better knowing that everything you see is real?" Amber had asked.

"I don't know. The little I've seen of this city is weird. Here, my laboratory is in a large, clean building, but elsewhere you have old and, frankly, dirty houses. And the people are noisy and, how can I say it, unconventional."

"We are real people, you know? That's what it is."

"Sometimes it scares me," he had said, and then he had become distant and reticent.

He was more relaxed in the lab. There he was in his element, and Amber gave up nudging him to go outside. Instead, she would sit and listen to his explanations of obscure technical facts that went straight over her head. He seemed to enjoy telling her about his work, and she found his enthusiasm to be contagious.

On the day when everything changed, Amber walked into the laboratory without knocking. Kal was peering at a screen, and she watched him in silence. He liked being alone when he was working. Amber had only been able to sneak in short visits, which she usually spent forcing him to eat.

"Hey!" she said when he failed to acknowledge her presence.

Her relationship with Kal was complex and still quite depressing to her. Outwardly, he was the same Kal with whom she had become close and comfortable. Sometimes she forgot that his memory was gone and that all the friendship and intimacy she felt was one-sided. Not that he wasn't friendly, but he was often distant and unresponsive. He was usually unsmiling and seldom relaxed, but now he turned toward her with a welcoming expression that changed into a broad, happy smile.

"It works!" he said.

"You made it?" Amber cried with excitement.

"I did. I can't test it on myself now that I am chipless, but all the tests I ran on my models show it works. I'm sure that I will be able to neutralize the effect of the augmented reality broadcast in a wide area."

"How wide?"

"I'm not sure yet. I'll have to test it in the field, but it's going to be pretty wide."

"We need to call Afex right away," said Amber.

"We will, but let's sit down for a few minutes first. I've been so busy that we haven't had the time to talk for a while now. How are you doing?"

Amber seated herself beside him on the long lab bench. There were so many screens and keyboards that they occupied almost the entire length of the room.

"I'm okay. I'm worried about my father's fate. We don't get much news about him, but he wasn't doing well the last I heard. They had to take him to a hospital, I don't know why. I wish we could use your technology to free him."

"We will, I promise. We will free everybody in The City from the High Professor, and we will get your father back. It's only a matter of time."

"I wish I could be as optimistic as you. I'm afraid that time is running out for my father."

They sat in silence for a long minute, and then Kal averted his gaze.

"You know that I don't sleep a lot. I've had strong headaches. The doctor says they will pass, but it may take some time. Still, when I manage to sleep, I dream strange dreams."

"Strange like what?"

"Like me doing things that don't feel like me. Tell me," he asked, "before I got hurt ... did I like you?"

"You said you did. I know you did," she whispered.

"I can't remember," said Kal, regret in his voice. "Did you like me?"

"I did. A lot. I do." It was Amber's turn to look away in embarrassment.

"I'm going to call Afex." Kal jumped up and strode across the room to the communication center.

——— · — · ———

Freeland's best technical teams had worked nonstop for thirty hours. Kal's equipment was now secured to one of the few working flying platforms that Freeland still operated. Kal was inspecting it like a proud father, and Afex and Amber had given up trying to dissuade him from flying with it. His argument that he had to monitor the results and make appropriate adjustments was clearly sound.

"You'll be careful," instructed Afex.

"I will, don't worry."

"If your system works, you may create havoc in New City. I don't know exactly what, but it may get things moving and set off a chain reaction. I've got all our reserve military forces on standby in case things deteriorate. Still, I worry that they may attack your platform if they discover it. After all, it's a vulnerable vehicle," said Afex.

"I thought about that, and I have a solution. The chips in the heads of our enemies are the ace in our sleeve. I didn't tell you until now, because I wasn't sure that it would work, but now I am. I have found a way to modulate an additional signal on the one that neutralizes The City's augmented reality broadcast. My lab tests predict that it will work."

"Do you mean that you'll be able to create an augmented reality of your own?"

"Exactly. I have prepared a few images that I am sure will modulate well. When the people down in New City see them, it'll take their minds off us, I can assure you. They'll be busy trying to avoid falling into wide cracks in the ground or being grabbed by giant flying insects. I've made those highly directional, so I don't need to inflict them on the general population. The others will simply be freed from the illusion broadcast by The City. And then, of course, there is the service announcement that I'll broadcast to everybody via the regular open channel used by The City."

"Let me see that again," said Afex.

Citizens of New City, it said, *you have been used by The City's tyrants and fooled into believing a false reality. What you see now outside is the real world. The chip has made you see things that do not exist, and we have canceled the illusion created by The City, so you can see for yourselves that what we say is true. We, your friends of Freeland, came to free you from the slavery of the chip, so you can see reality for what it is. This is a sample. We are not plotting against you. Your own government is. Look outside, and you'll see. Now it's time to revolt against the tyranny of The City. They armed you to fight us, and you can turn those weapons against them. Now it's time for you to join the free world. We will welcome you with open arms. Repeat with us: "No more chip!"*

"Forceful," Afex commented. "Of course, we don't know how the people of New City will react. They may believe that it is all a trick organized by Freeland and hate us even more."

"But if we don't try it, we will never know what effect it may have on the population of The City, right, Uncle?" said Amber.

"Correct. It is risky, but it will be like a big laboratory experiment. If the people of New City react well to our message, then we will have something we can use against The City itself."

"Time to go," said Kal.

"I'm coming with you." Amber took a step forward, leaving Afex's side.

"No way!" said Afex.

"It's too dangerous," said Kal.

"Try and stop me." Amber's expression left no doubt that she meant it.

Afex sighed.

"I've failed before, trying to convince you to stay behind. I won't make a fool of myself again," he said.

"Thank you, Uncle," said Amber.

"Are you sure? I have to be there, but you don't have to," said Kal. "In fact, you can't help me in any way, so why risk it?"

"Don't be too cocky, presuming that you don't need me. I've saved your neck before, and I may have to do it again. Who knows what kind of trouble you will land yourself in this time? Now let's go."

Kal nodded and didn't attempt to protest again. Together they stepped on the gangway leading to the flying platform and boarded. Afex stood and watched as the pilot started the engine and then maneuvered away.

"We'll be approaching New City soon," said the pilot.

"Good. Give us a heads up a few minutes before. We'll be on the upper deck, making sure that all the equipment is ready," said Kal.

Amber and Kal climbed the stairs to the upper deck. Kal examined his equipment again and again before going to stand by the window. The night sky was clear, and the scenery beneath them was breathtaking. They watched the buildings disappear under them. Then they flew above treetops and rolling grass.

"It's so beautiful!" said Amber. "I wonder if we'll make it back. I know that this is a dangerous mission, and if anything bad happens, I want—"

"Amber," Kal interrupted her. "I know that this is not the best time, but I wanted to tell you that I'm remembering things."

"Yes? Like what?" Amber's heart started beating faster as Kal got closer. She waited for him to go on.

"I'm not sure. I remember us traveling in a truck, and a little boy was with us," he said.

"Yes! That was Tim. I didn't tell you about him. I will. That means that you are getting your memory back." Amber could not curb her excitement.

"Don't get too excited," Kal admonished her. "I don't remember much else. Give me your hand," he added, "I'm trying to capture a feeling."

Amber took his hand and pressed it. Until then, Kal had made sure to avoid physical contact, and his asking for it had to mean he was improving.

"New City ahead!" boomed the captain's voice over the intercom.

"Shit!" said Amber as Kal dropped her hand and ran to turn on his equipment.

CHAPTER 37

New City resident Tom Ketchum was proud of the role assigned to him in the defense of his people. He was an appointed squad leader and owned a modern ray gun. He knew that he would act with courage and determination when the time came to fight the odious Freelanders. He would lead his men in defense of his city and of his family. He had been fast asleep only a moment before, but now something had woken him. His wife stood by the window, crying.

"What's the matter? What happened?" he inquired. His wife was strong-minded and rational and never given to erratic behavior like this.

"Outside. Look outside!" she cried, and then she crouched on the floor.

Worried and astonished, Ketchum ran to the window. What could be so scary in the nice pasture view they saw from their window? He stared out and couldn't believe his eyes: gone were the trees and the grass; instead, only sand, stones, and small boulders filled the view.

"What happened? Am I going mad?" he cried.

"Listen!" said his wife.

A voice spoke in his head. *Citizens of New City*, it said, *you have been used by The City's tyrants and fooled into believing a false reality.* He listened to the announcement and then listened to it again. His wife ran to the other room and returned with their three-year-old daughter.

"What are we going to do?" she asked, crying and holding her daughter in her arms.

Before Ketchum could respond, a voice boomed from the loudspeakers that dotted the complex. "The invasion is beginning," it said. "It's time to arm ourselves and fight back. All squad leaders must assemble their men in full combat gear and be ready to march on Freeland to fight the invader."

But Ketchum wasn't paying attention to it. He was too busy listening again and again to the announcement that came over the chip channel. Every time he heard it, the message sounded truer and more convincing. He put on his combat gear and took his ray gun.

"Stay here," he said to his wife and walked outside.

Squad leaders were assembling their men behind them in the large esplanade outside. Housing complex 17—the one assigned to Ketchum's family—was built around that esplanade. At the square center, next to the statue of the High Professor, the City-appointed governor of New City complex 17 waited, flanked by four military instructors.

"You're responding well. Good for you! I commend you! All 57 New City complexes report responding at the same speed. We are proud of you." He shouted so everybody could hear, "The time has come to act. You have been well-trained to defend your home and your family from the enemy. As soon as every able-bodied person answers the call, we will mount our vehicles and start our attack on the so-called Freeland. You know your roles, and the orders are to take no prisoners."

"What is happening to our land?" called Ketchum.

"You know what's happening. The enemy is spreading disease and destruction. It is ruining the land around us to rob us of our dreams," the New City appointee recited.

"But where have all the grass and the trees outside our perimeter gone? Why is it that all we can see is a desert? You've been lying to us!" Ketchum accused him.

Loud cries of "Yes!" and "Explain!" came from the crowd. The governor conferred in a low voice with the instructors, and as they turned to face the crowd, two of them pointed their guns at Ketchum. But he was quicker. His weapon, which he had turned on before by releasing the safety catch, fired first. The blast sent the governor backward against the statue and then to the floor. Other guns fired, and soon all instructors were down.

"This way, to the governor's mansion!" Ketchum cried, and many in the large crowd followed him. They were shouting, "No more chip!" and the chant began to resound throughout New City.

———

Back at headquarters, Afex watched the image of New City that Kal's flying platform relayed to him. Flames were visible, coming from the governor's mansion. Kal and Amber stood on the bridge, looking at the scene in awe.

"It worked; you did it!" Afex cried with overt excitement over the communication channel. "You gave us a way to neutralize the most powerful tool that The City has to control its citizens. This is huge!"

"Do you hear it, Uncle?" Amber asked.

"Hear what?"

"The chant coming from New City."

"Keep quiet, and perhaps I'll hear it."

They remained silent for a minute, and then Afex's emotional voice came through the communication system again.

"I think ... I think they're singing 'No more chip.' Is that what they're saying?"

"Yes, it is," said Kal. He switched off the communication system, and Afex's image disappeared, leaving a dark screen.

"Why did you do that?" Amber asked.

"I needed privacy. I want to talk to you. As I told you, I am starting to remember, but the details are elusive, and I don't want to lose those memories again. I remember having feelings that were new to me ...."

"What kind of feelings?"

"I have a vision of us talking. When I see it, I feel strange. It's kind of unreal."

"And?"

"And in my vision, we are close, touching."

"Like this?" Amber asked. She took his hand and pulled him close, gently, until their bodies touched.

Kal swallowed and nodded in assent.

"I'm remembering, but it's confusing. Tell me everything once more, from the beginning. It helps me when you talk to me."

Amber started to tell him again, with as many details as she remembered, without letting go of his hand. She had reached the point where they had to cross the underground river when the captain's voice boomed over the intercom again.

"The chairman needs to speak with you," he said.

"Yes, Afex," said Kal, after turning the communication system on again.

"Come back at once," said Afex. He looked clearly preoccupied.

"What's the matter, Uncle?" Amber asked.

"I got word that The City launched its fleet. Not hard to guess which way they are going. I need you back in one piece, Kal."

"It's starting!" Amber said.

"We're coming," said Kal. He switched the communication system off again.

"Leave it on," Amber suggested.

"You don't want me to," said Kal, smiling.

REWIRED (BOOK 2) — CHAPTER 1 PREVIEW

CHAPTER 1

Amber gazed at the young people assembled in the auditorium. They were all cadets, eager to learn from the mouth of someone who had been in The City. The lectures that she had agreed to give under the "know your enemy" doctrine always took her back to her days with Kal. They reminded her of the dangers they faced together but also of the excitement of self-discovery.

"So let's recap what we have learned today. The story taught in The City is that since the Pulse, the biology of humans and animals has diverged so much that one could be dangerous to the other. Therefore, The City had erected an invisible barrier to prevent birds and other flying creatures from entering it and contaminating the environment. It is also completely sealed by a physical barrier that keeps animals out and humans inside. Still, it is some consolation for the citizens that they can watch nature, even if only from afar. This narrative, false as it is, is what keeps the citizens of The City enslaved, although they don't realize it."

"I don't get it," a boy in the front row murmured. "Are they stupid or what?"

"The citizens see pastoral scenes, with animals grazing in green pastures and birds fluttering all around. Unfortunately, they don't really exist; they see augmented reality broadcast to their brains by the chip. If the augmented reality signal is taken away, and their chips stop creating the illusion, all they see around The City is dry, scorched ground, and not a live creature in sight."

"But they don't see it … I get it now," the boy said.

"The citizens are told that they owe their happiness to Alvin, the High Professor. He is the genius who perfected the chip implanted in every citizen's brain on their first birthday. He had taken the initial prototype, developed by the first High Professor in the decades following The Pulse, and turned it into the technological marvel it is today. Thanks to the chip, everything in The City runs smoothly and in an orderly fashion. Crime has disappeared, and nobody is helpless anymore. If anything bad happens to you or your body, help is immediately available, right there in your head. What's more, thanks to the chip, you always know the right thing to do and the correct way to go."

"Is that for real?" a girl in the second row wondered.

"Of course not. There is always a little truth in all lies, but fundamentally, it's a lie. That's what Kal discovered one day when his chip malfunctioned. For a moment, the nice images that the chip projected to his brain, what we call 'augmented reality,' disappeared, and all he saw was desolation. He then realized that the sheep, the grass, and the birds were all the fruit of imagination."

"But why would the rulers do that?" the girl insisted.

"Because The City is dying. Before The Pulse, more than nineteen million people lived there. Now it's less than three million. The ruling caste, led by the so-called High Professor, is recycling the dwindling resources of The City. They keep The City going with goods they get from outside and keep all contacts with the outside world secret. I was lucky to meet Kal on the same day he discovered all that; otherwise, I would probably not be here to tell you about it."

The Kal she had met was different from the man he was today, she reminded herself. But she had to push thoughts of Kal away; it was too distracting.

"So, to wrap this up, my original mission to The City was a failure. I had gone there to try to rescue my father, who was and still is a prisoner of the High Professor. That changed when Kal revolted after he discovered how the chip implanted in every citizen one year after birth makes him a slave and keeps him from seeing reality as it is. I had friends in The City who had agreed to help me with my mission. After Kal turned up, they convinced me to abandon my personal mission and instead guide him here. Getting here wasn't easy, and we almost got killed on the way, more than once. Kal was in the direst danger. The chip is set up so it will melt, killing its owner, if it doesn't receive the signal broadcast in The City for two full weeks, and that's how Kal almost died here. It was just luck that we got him to Freeland in time."

"You're awesome!" one of the girls sitting in the last row said. "Freeland owes you and Kal a lot."

"Well, this hasn't turned out as well as we had hoped. As you know, New City was The City's outpost close to here, and we hoped to make them see the truth and join us in the fight against The City's tyrants. Kal managed to neutralize the virtual reality signal that kept New City's citizens slaves and ready to fight us, but didn't realize that this would provoke a carnage. The City sent its fleet to destroy New City and kill its rogue settlers."

"Still, New City was a threat to us before, wasn't it?" asked a boy sitting in the front row.

"Yes, it was, and perhaps our fight with The City will be easier without them, but it may happen sooner than we expected, and that's why we are here. Time's up," she added. These lectures drained her of all her emotional energy, and she was eager to end this one.

The cadets, almost 200 of them, were older than she–perhaps only one or two years older, but somehow, after everything she had gone through, they looked like children to her. They were teenagers whose lives were about to be thrown into the horrors of war without really knowing what war was about. She hated the eagerness with which they prepared for it, but she couldn't help admiring it, coming from boys and girls who had grown up in a free and open society. She had let her mind wander, and a question brought her back to the present from her musings.

"Understanding the difference between City people and us is not easy," she said, answering the question. "The society they live in is not based on free will but on a distorted conception of what is good for the individual. All choices are made for them, even the smallest ones, like what to eat, when to eat, and what to read. Human intercourse is also minimal and regulated. The chip does all the work for them. If you have one implanted in your head, it tells you what and who is right for you."

"So, if I want to ask you out, I need to ask permission of the chip?" one of the boys asked, followed by giggles from the crowd.

"You don't ask anybody out," Amber said, speaking somberly.

"When the time comes to procreate, The City's management will let you know who your selected partner is."

"But," the boy insisted, "how can they stop two people who like each other from getting together? It's only natural ..."

"There is nothing natural about it. The chip suppresses everybody's natural instincts until it is time to procreate. Then and only then the chip gives them the stimuli needed to do it," said Amber.

"We should put a chip in your head," a girl said, laughing, to the boy who had spoken.

"But then you would look for the button that turns on the stimuli twice a day," the boy retorted, and the whole auditorium burst into a loud laugh.

Amber couldn't conceal a smile, but then she forced herself to turn serious again. "It is actually not that funny," she said. "People who grow up like that are like machines, lacking a will to live life as we know it. And in the rare cases in which they managed to free themselves from the tyranny of the chip, they have a tough time when they need to make decisions for themselves."

"Can you tell us how it was for you and Kal once he was no longer under the influence of the chip?"

A girl sitting in the first row had asked the question and was looking at Amber expectantly.

"We need not discuss Kal. We want to respect his privacy. He deserves it also, but not only because of the great debt that Freeland owes him."

"Do you love him?" the girl insisted.

"We have run out of time, so this is it until next week," said Amber, speaking tonelessly. The cadets got up quickly, and in less than a minute, the auditorium was empty. Amber stood there, facing the empty seats, lost in thought.

"Did she love him?" she asked herself, perhaps for the thousandth time. "Hell, yes!" she answered herself again. But life was too complicated, and the balance was too delicate to allow her to translate those feelings into words.

Amber walked the long corridors of Headquarters with a confidence that was always apparent in her gait. She felt strong and a sense of belonging in her uniform, with the double chevron that identified her as an officer. The Chief of Staff, who had pinned them on her shoulders, had assured her that she had earned them. She needed that reassurance because of her uncle's position as Chairman of Freeland's Council and her fear that people around her would think that nepotism was behind her promotion. However, as time passed, she realized she had earned the people's respect through her actions and nothing else.

Being Afex's niece still had its advantages that Amber sometimes accepted with remorse. After all, it had opened the door for her to Earl, the Chief Psychology Officer, whose help she really needed. His office was at the end of the corridor. She knocked lightly on the door, pushing it open when the words "come in" were shouted from within.

"Ah, Amber, good to see you; I was waiting for you," said Earl, with a welcoming smile.

Earl was tall, a full head taller than Amber, with full black hair and pale blue eyes. Amber estimated him to be around 40 years old. His movements made it clear that he was in perfect physical shape. He was cleanly shaven, with a face that inspired confidence and a demeanor that instantly created a relaxed atmosphere. He got up to greet her, gesturing for her to sit in one of the two seats that stood before his desk. Then he came to sit next to her on the other one, immediately creating a relaxed, fatherly atmosphere. That was a well-known knack of his.

"You're here because of Kal, aren't you? Afex said that you're worried," he added when she nodded. "What can I do for you?"

"I ... I don't know what to do. Just before the attack on New City, it seemed he was regaining his memory, and we were bonding again. Before we left for our flight to New City, he was distant and didn't remember almost anything we'd been through together. But then, when we were there alone, flying toward our dangerous mission, and then back, something changed. He positively told me that he was remembering, and he no longer avoided touching me. But now, it is like he has 'switched off' again. I don't understand it, and I don't know what to do or what's right. Since I joined the Defense Corps, I haven't seen much of him, and I think he has been avoiding me. Please tell me what to do."

"It's not easy, you know. I don't have all the answers either. When Kal's chip went into self-destruction mode, his brain was damaged. The damage was not great but was enough to erase part of his memory and destabilize his behavioral patterns. It's not surprising that he is vulnerable and prone to mood swings."

"But what can be done?"

"I am treating him, so I shouldn't be discussing his condition with you or anybody else. However, I will make an exception because I think you can help him a great deal. But what I'm going to tell you must remain between us."

"Anything you say!"

Earl took a quick glance at the door to make sure that it was closed and lowered his voice.

"Kal is blaming himself for what happened to New City, for all the deaths and destruction. In my opinion, this is the reason for his regression. And, in all fairness, it was his technology that forced The City's hand. He was the one who found the way to cancel the augmented reality signal created by The City officials who ran New City. As a result, he forced everyone to see the real world they lived in. After realizing that they had been lied to and made fools of, it was inevitable that the population of New City would revolt. It was our mistake that we didn't budget for the swift action that The City was obliged to take as a result."

"But Kal couldn't have known that! He can't blame himself for it," Amber protested.

"But he does, perhaps not so much consciously, but deep

down, he feels that he is to blame, and that made him retreat into himself."

"So, what can I do to help him?"

"He needs a new purpose. It must be something with a positive goal, and he must convince himself that it is for a worthy cause. You must lead him to it."

"Why me?"

"It is my professional opinion, after spending many hours with him, that he has strong feelings for you. I don't know to what extent he realizes it, but those feelings are deep-seated. If someone can help him climb out of the hole into which he has dug himself, you are that person."

"I'll do what I can—anything … everything," said Amber, almost choking on her words.

"I know that. That's why I agreed to talk to you. I've done all I can for Kal, and I no longer seem to make progress. It's in your hands now," said Earl. "You need to find a way to motivate him, but I am afraid that I can't help you with it. By the way, this conversation we just had—it never happened."

He got up, circled his desk, and sat behind it, signaling that the discussion was concluded.

Amber stood up in silence, nodded to show she understood, and walked out with leaden feet. The weight of the responsibility that Earl had placed on her shoulders was almost unbearable.

THANK YOU FOR READING

I hope you enjoyed the journey.

If you have a moment, I'd be grateful if you left a brief review at the retailer where you purchased it. Even a few words can make a real difference and help me continue bringing new stories to readers like you.

Thank you for your support.

— Kfir Luzzatto

JOIN MY READER COMMUNITY

Want to know when my next book is released?

Join my reader community and receive updates about new releases, special promotions, and exclusive content available only to subscribers.

Sign up here:

https://www.kfirluzzatto.com/about
I look forward to staying in touch.

— Kfir Luzzatto

MEET THE AUTHOR

Kfir Luzzatto is the author of eighteen novels, several short stories, and seven non-fiction books. Kfir was born and raised in Italy and moved to Israel as a teenager. He acquired his love for the English language from his father, a former U.S. soldier, a voracious reader, and a prolific writer. He holds a Ph.D. in chemical engineering and works as a patent attorney. In pursuit of his interest in the mind-body connection, Kfir was certified as a Clinical Hypnotherapist by the Anglo-European College of Therapeutic Hypnosis.

Kfir is a member of the HWA (Horror Writers Association) and ITW (International Thriller Writers). You can visit Kfir's website and read his blog at https://www.kfirluzzatto.com/. Follow him on X (@KfirLuzzatto) and friend him on Facebook (https://www.-facebook.com/KfirLuzzattoAuthor).

ALSO BY KFIR LUZZATTO

ENCODED MINDS

PARALLELS

CROSSING THE MEADOW

THE ODYSSEY GENE

THE EVELYN PROJECT

HAVE BOOK, WILL TRAVEL
(With Yonatan Luzzatto)

AN ITALIAN OBSESSION

EXODUS '95

CHIPLESS

REWIRED (*The sequel to CHIPLESS*)

ONCE AWAKENED

The Tessa Extra-Sensory Agent series:

TESSA (Tessa Extra-Sensory Agent Book 1)

THE OTHERS (Tessa Extra-Sensory Agent Book 2)

HUNTER (Tessa Extra-Sensory Agent Book 3)

PHANTOM (Tessa Extra-Sensory Agent Book 4)

RUNNER (Tessa Extra-Sensory Agent Book 5)

VENETIAN (Tessa Extra-Sensory Agent Book 6)

MAFIOSA (Tessa Extra-Sensory Agent, Book 7)

The Young Telepath series
(Adapted from the TESSA series for young adults.)

The DEAD & BUSY series:

#1: ACCIDENTAL LAZARUS

#2: PHANTOM LOVER

#3: MICE

#4: THE ACCOUNTANT

Short Story Collections:

HIS DARKER SIDE

HIS LIGHTER SIDE

www.ingramcontent.com/pod-product-compliance
Lightning Source LLC
Chambersburg PA
CBHW031720170626
46808CB00005B/1818